PRAISE FOR

ERIC LAROCCA

"LaRocca is a writer to watch."
—*Publisher's Weekly*

"Eric LaRocca is considered the Beethoven of queer horror, composing nuanced queer stories that really touch a chord."
—*Them*

"LaRocca proves himself a fresh voice in horror and one more than capable of pulling us into his uniquely visceral imagination."
—*Rue Morgue*

"Eric LaRocca has conjured for us a mad, beautiful tale of dark magic, trauma and love, and how these things intertwine—this is an author in command of powerful narrative sorceries, and is deserving of your immediate attention."
—Chuck Wendig, author of *The Book of Accidents*

"*Everything the Darkness Eats* is an emotionally devastating novel of unflinching violence, lost souls, and cosmic horror. Eric LaRocca's prose sings and his characters are heart-achingly true. Another brilliant work from one of horror's fastest-rising talents."
—Tim Waggoner, author of *We Will Rise* and *Your Turn to Suffer*

"A colossal feat of imagination and moments of pure magic delivered with style and tenderness in a way that gives Gaiman a run for his money."
—Gemma Amor, author of *Dear Laura* and *Full Immersion*

"After already conquering short stories and novellas, it should be no surprise that more Eric LaRocca is even better. With his novel-length debut, he promises us a feast fit for Darkness itself, and, my God, does he deliver."
—Nat Cassidy, author of *Mary: An Awakening of Terror*

EVERY-THING THE DARKNESS EATS

ERIC LAROCCA

A NOVEL

TROY, NY

CLASH Books
www.clashbooks.com
Troy, NY

For my mother.
I don't believe. But she does.
I wrote this book for her.

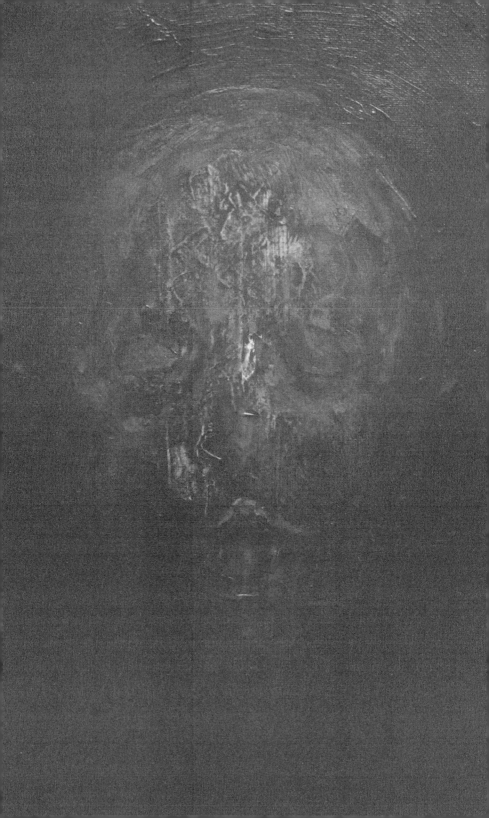

"Is he able, but not willing? Then he is malevolent."
—Epicurus

PROLOGUE

Wales, 1994 A.D.

It was late in the afternoon on the third day in April when the Excavation Director—a large man with a pockmarked face named Mr. Pritchard—sent his nine-year-old son to fetch Heart Crowley and tell him they had found something.

Mr. Pritchard told his son that he would most likely find Mr. Crowley taking his afternoon tea, as was his custom, in the small tent they had constructed at the foot of the mountain—not only a place of refuge from the icy wind, but a sanctuary where they could catalog the artifacts they had uncovered.

If you could even call them artifacts, that is.

Nearly two weeks at the dig site and hardly any of the items they had unearthed were unfit to appear in even the most tasteless sideshow attraction.

But finally—a sign.

Mr. Pritchard's son scampered down the path, mountain wind

beating hard against him and spiriting him further ahead as if he were being carried by an invisible gloved hand. When he came to the tent, he peered inside and found the room empty—maps strewn across the tables, digging tools left unguarded. As he circled the tent, he came upon a small embankment and stared down into it only to find Mr. Crowley on his knees sifting through a large tray of dirt.

"Mr. Crowley," the boy called, waving his arms in the air. "They found something."

Mr. Crowley was on his feet in a matter of seconds, climbing up the small ridge. As he approached, the boy couldn't help but notice how much older Mr. Crowley seemed to appear despite his age—his mouth constantly pulling downward, the swollen pouches of excess skin beneath each of his eyes. He resembled something not unlike a fresh cadaver that had yet to become smartened by a skilled mortician.

The boy began to lead Mr. Crowley further up the mountain path toward the rim where most of the excavation crew had gathered. As they neared the summit, the young boy turned and noticed Mr. Crowley's pace slowing to a crawl, his eyes seemingly transfixed by the neighboring mountains curtained with low-hanging mist—the primordial landscape screaming at the both of them as a rainstorm shower passed over.

Finally reaching the ridge where the crew was waiting, the young boy watched as Mr. Crowley greeted Mr. Pritchard with a look of uncertainty. Mr. Pritchard merely passed a helmet to Mr. Crowley and motioned for him to venture inside the small crevice they had opened in the nearby patchwork of boulders.

The boy filed inside the small chamber after the others had

followed Mr. Crowley and Mr. Pritchard. Flashlights tore bright glowing halos in the darkness, the walls shimmering wet and viscous looking like the black, oiled skin of some underwater creature.

"Where is it?" Mr. Crowley asked the director, panting like a dog in heat from his recent climb.

His way of asking seemed more akin to a petulant toddler seeking gifts on a holiday than a benefactor who had sunk nearly half of his savings into funding this dig.

Mr. Pritchard answered, aiming his flashlight at a section of the wall in front of them. "Look."

Mr. Crowley's eyes followed the pool of light and arrived at a primitive drawing etched into the rock. Although it might have been rudimentary in construction when compared with the Sistine Chapel, the illustration was gloriously ornate in design. It was an etching of a group of people standing in a circle as if in worship, a bright light at the center of their gathering and a giant shape—a creator—sprawling from the middle of the light. Ancient hieroglyphics and other symbols were scrawled beneath the illustration and resembled the vague outline of a prayer.

Mr. Pritchard's son watched as Mr. Crowley's mouth hung open. He watched him press his trembling hands against the wall, his eyes sparkling wet and shining.

"You found it," Mr. Crowley whispered.

The boy watched as his father flanked Mr. Crowley and wiped the dirt from his brow with a small handkerchief.

"What is it?" Mr. Pritchard asked.

Mr. Crowley inhaled deeply through his nostrils, drawing in thousand-year-old oxygen, and seeming to straighten at a newfound vitality coursing through him.

"It's an invocation."

Mr. Crowley's eyes snapped to Mr. Pritchard and seemed to widen with hideous intent. Mr. Pritchard's face furrowed, quizzically studying him when suddenly he seemed incapacitated. Mr. Crowley's stare intensified until Mr. Pritchard dropped to his knees, the poor man's body convulsing as if in the throes of a grand mal seizure.

Some of the other excavation crew members tried to hasten to his rescue, but Mr. Crowley merely raised a hand and commanded them to halt. They obeyed, their eyes dimming and glazing over as if hypnotized.

The boy watched helplessly as Mr. Crowley circled his half-dead prey. Mr. Pritchard's body seized and spasmed like a drowning insect.

Finally, with the flick of his wrist, Mr. Crowley seemed to command Mr. Pritchard to explode—bright scarlet ribbons fountaining from the gaping hole he had opened where the man's head once was. Mr. Pritchard's headless body slumped to the ground like a discarded child's toy, his clothing dyed dark red as more blood pumped from the severed wellspring deep inside him.

Mr. Crowley turned on the other diggers—waving his hand at them and exploding each of their heads as if they were mere balloons. Heads burst like swollen sacks of meat tethered to dynamite, blood splattering the cave walls and dripping like fresh paint. Headless bodies tumbled forward, arms flailing helplessly as if attempting to undo what could never be undone.

When he was finished with the others, Mr. Crowley cornered the boy where the two walls met.

The boy did not cry or plead with him.

Instead, he sank to his knees and merely waited for it to be over—for the dome of his skull to mushroom like a nocturnal plant in twilight's bloom and to be swallowed by thought as red as sunset.

PART ONE

A SCARECROW AFTER
A SUMMER STORM

"Every angel is terrifying."
—Rainer Maria Rilke, *Duino Elegies*

CHAPTER ONE

Present Day

I f by some inexplicable force of sorcery, Ghost Everling's skin suddenly became as transparent as a sheet of cellophane, the young man wouldn't even consider objecting. He wouldn't seek out a cure, wouldn't consult with physicians or skin specialists to remedy his peculiar ailment. He wouldn't even act surprised or feign terror the way others might.

For Ghost, invisibility had already claimed him long ago.

He conceded there was something uniquely strange that occurred when you lost a loved one. Something that wasn't in the literature he had read in despair or the self-help podcasts he had listened to on his morning walks throughout his neighborhood. Something that had hollowed him out and rendered him as "unusable goods" to any woman or man that would have him.

Although it had only been three years since his wife, Hailey, had passed, Ghost figured he knew all there was to know about invisibility. More specifically, he knew all there was to know about being left behind—the phone calls of condolences from family that became less and less frequent, the friends that had shied away from him as if fearful they might be touched by the same sorrow too. Everyone around him seemed to move on, while Ghost remained trapped in place.

Yes, trapped.

Ghost knew everything there was to know about traps, too.

Some of them don't appear until later in life, as if secreted beneath underbrush like the iron mouthpiece of a hunter's snare.

He couldn't go a day without glancing in the mirror and being reminded of the trap that had demanded his body three years ago—a wraith of guilt wrapped around his neck the way an infant chimpanzee clings to its mother. He could scarcely forget the moment when he first realized it was there—a thin wisp of white smoke curling about his throat, claws of vapor as finely delicate as Chantilly lace plugging his nose and ears.

From there, it only grew.

Although invisible to others, the tiny nymph-like parasite constantly made itself known to Ghost. Whether it was ladling thoughts of despair into his mind or suckling from the roots of sadness it had planted deep inside him, the spirit clung to its gracious host without thanks and the two lived as if they were one—as if they were somehow welded together by some complex, invisible arrangement made of bone and any separation would prove fatal.

Ghost seldom complained when the tiny spirit that owned him would nest inside the scar across his face that never healed—a dark line, rusted brown with dried blood, as though he had been struck by lightning. He hardly had the energy to object when his little companion would circle his permanently bloodshot right eye, coiling in there and lazing like an earthworm in a bed of dirt.

For Ghost, his body was nothing more than a compost heap—a crude patchwork of abused anatomy that even the most impulsive surrealist wouldn't dare commemorate on canvas. Ghost knew full well he was a monster, a horrible mutation handmade by grief. At least much of the sorrow he carried was invisible to most.

He thanked God for that.

After washing himself and drinking his morning coffee, Ghost swiped his cane from the coat rack and limped out to the garage where his old Chevrolet had remained parked and lifeless for the past three years. He eased himself into the driver's seat and sat there for a moment, swirling the keys in his hands and deliberating whether or not to use them.

Of course, he had had the dreadful thought before—jamming the keys into the ignition and waiting for the garage bay to fill with smoke while he gasped for air. Something in him had whispered that it would be painless, that he would be reunited with his love and all would be forgiven—all would be as it had been before. However, there was a smaller, quieter part of him that had challenged him, that had warned him it would be pointless because, even to God, Ghost was invisible.

If that was the case, where would he go? Ghost certainly never wanted to find out.

After calling the local taxi company and waiting for half an hour, a yellow cab pulled onto the lane's shoulder and idled in front of his house. Propped up by his cane, Ghost limped out to the cab.

exchanged a few polite greetings with the driver and then directed him to the Henley's Edge Memorial Hospital.

As he sat in the backseat, he gazed out the window and watched as they passed people and houses he had known all his life—things he had once found comfort in for the mere sake of their familiarity. But somehow the houses began to look different, as if brick, stone, and stucco had been miraculously replaced with rubber or elastic—as if they were slowly melting away like burning candles. Even the people he once knew looked strange, memorable faces now thawing until almost unrecognizable as if forever caught in a blurred snapshot.

Ghost had quickly realized that grief had not only changed him but had remade the world the same way a child might manhandle a clump of wet clay.

Although things in the town of Henley's Edge hardly ever changed, the way in which Ghost saw certain things could never be undone.

It wasn't long before the taxi pulled up to the hospital entrance, Ghost tipping the driver with a few extra dollars before climbing out of the idling car and limping into the already packed waiting room. Passing through rows of chairs filled with patients, Ghost approached the front desk and was greeted by a petite receptionist with a face caked with so much makeup that only an embalmed cadaver could compare.

"Name," she barked at him.

"Ghost Everling."

"How do you spell it?" she asked, fingers already flicking across her computer keyboard.

"Like the thing that goes 'boo.'"

The receptionist scowled at him, clearly not amused. "What seems to be the trouble?"

"I came here last week because I kept getting these intense headaches," he explained, shoving his index finger between his front teeth out of nervous habit. "They gave me some meds for it, but they've started up again and I'm getting a little concerned. This is the second time this month and I just want to be sure it's not something serious."

The receptionist grabbed a nearby clipboard and pen and slid them across the counter toward Ghost.

"Fill this out," she said, snatching the phone as it rang and pressing it against her ear. "We'll be right with you."

The tiny spirit perched on Ghost's shoulder orbited his head for a moment and then pulled his ear down to its mouth.

"She probably thinks you're just another pathetic junkie," the spirit hissed at Ghost until he swatted it away, its shapeless form dissolving as if it were made of wet cotton.

The little wraith rematerialized not long after, sprouting from beside Ghost's other shoulder and whispering into his ear: "Looking to score some dope. Typical trash."

Ghost, face heating red, glanced back at the receptionist, as if fearful she had somehow heard.

She couldn't have.

But what if she did? He worried.

"I'm not looking for new meds or anything like that," he assured her, sensing the muscles in his throat flexing as he swallowed nervously. "I'm just—I just want to make sure everything's OK."

The receptionist stared at him blankly, perhaps more annoyed than anything else. "Sir, have a seat. We'll be right with you."

Of course, it wasn't the assurance Ghost had longed for, but it would have to do for now. The little spirit was hardly tempered, winging about his head the same way blackflies circle a horse's snout.

Ghost retreated from the front desk and found an empty seat near the waiting room window. Glancing up from his clipboard, his eyes were caught by a young mother and daughter seated across from him.

The little girl was perhaps no older than seven or eight—a frightening age as the nightmarish specter of adolescence hangs just overhead. He reasoned that innocence had already deserted the poor child as he saw the girl's arm had been broken and bound in a cast scrawled with messages and drawings from her friends and family. Even worse, when she lifted her head, he noticed how both of her eyes were dim and clouded milky white. If any innocence remained in the poor child, it was as shriveled and as desiccated as a flower abandoned beneath a heat lamp.

Ghost marveled at her. There was something about the child, something that quietly told him she knew she was a monster just like him—something that confessed to him she felt invisible, too.

He watched her as she coveted a small balloon in the shape of a seahorse, looping the balloon's string around her index finger and pulling tight until the end of her finger was swollen blackish purple. He watched as she squeezed the balloon tighter and tighter until—POP.

She jumped, startled at the noise. Then, shrank and began to cry when she realized, as little tattered pieces of balloon showered her like confetti.

Ghost leaned forward in his seat, debating whether or not to intervene. He glanced at the mother, comforting her child while quietly fighting off disapproving scowls from loitering patients. Finally, his feet made the decision for him. Ghost staggered across the aisle and knelt in front of the child.

"There you are," he said. "I've been looking all over for you."

The little girl shrank from him, unsure. She clutched her mother's arm, sticking her thumb in her mouth.

"I was told there was a beautiful little princess somewhere here," Ghost said, wincing as he leaned against his cane for support. "I was told I had to give her three wishes."

He noticed how the child seemed to straighten, her face softening at the mention of the word "wishes." The corners of her mouth began to crease with a smile.

"What's your name?" he asked, glancing at the mother as if testing her comfort.

The little girl eased back in her chair, quiet. The mother tugged on her daughter's arm, smiling and urging her to play along.

"What's your name?" she asked her.

The little girl popped her thumb out of her mouth and flashed a wide, toothless grin. "Piper," she said.

"Princess Piper. That's exactly who I was told to find," Ghost said. "I'm so happy I found you because I think I have something you'll want."

Ghost flourished his cane, pushing the tip into the palm of Piper's hand so she could feel it.

"You see, I have what's known as a "magic stick." It grants wishes," he explained. "Three of them, to be precise. But the only trouble is— the wishes can't all be used at once. You have to spread them out."

Ghost glanced at the mother. She merely observed, amused.

"So, if you could have anything in the world right now—what would it be?" he asked her.

Piper considered the question for a moment, her lips moving quietly. "I'd want the doctor to hurry up, so my mommy and I don't have to wait so long."

Ghost simpered softly. Yes, perhaps there was some innocence remaining within her, after all. He thanked God for that. "Now, you have to rub the stick three times and say, "I believe.""

Ghost pressed his cane into Piper's hand, and she pushed her open palm against it three times. "I believe," she whispered.

Without warning, a grey-haired nurse entered the waiting room, her eyes squinting at her clipboard. "Piper?" she called out, scanning the room.

Ghost and Piper's mother locked eyes for an instant, the mother eyeing him with a look of "are you serious?" Piper leapt up from her seat, waving down the nurse until she finally approached them.

"I'm just going to take her height and weight," the nurse explained. "I'll bring her right back."

Grabbing Piper by the hand, the nurse guided Piper through aisles of waiting patients and steered her out of the waiting room.

Ghost gripped his cane, steadying himself and flinching as he rose from his knees.

"You're lucky she didn't wish for a pony," Piper's mother said. "She's been asking for one lately."

Ghost flashed an uncomfortable smile. "That's when you would've intervened, right?"

"You seemed to be doing fine just on your own." She offered her hand. "I'm Gemma."

Ghost took her hand, shaking it.

"Ghost," he said.

She looked at him queerly.

"Yes," he said. "Like Halloween."

Gemma stammered, unsure, as she guarded herself with politeness. "What an—unusual name."

"My mother's choice," Ghost explained. "Something she always thought of."

Gemma eyed him, as if he had stopped speaking mid-sentence. "Ghosts?"

Ghost lowered his head, turning away.

Of course, he was an expert in telling the story his mother had often told him when he was little—how on the night he was delivered, his mother claimed to have seen something: a spirit in the hospital room window. She had told him how the ghost was as blue as hydrangea, petals of its body dripping as if in the excruciating process of molting away. Perhaps the most unbelievable part of her story— how the spirit had told her that her child "belonged to them." Ghost had always wondered if that's why his mother was so protective of him when he was a child, as if fearful that he might be snatched away at any moment by some otherworldly trespasser.

Of course, he knew the story well, but he certainly didn't know Gemma well enough to tell her. She might have him committed. Besides, the way she looked at him, the way she studied his bloodshot eye, his permanent scar—all seemed to tell him that she couldn't quite make heads or tails of him. He was glad to be an enigma to her. He knew full well if he stayed longer, she would see him for what he truly was—a monster.

Just as he was about to excuse himself, she uncrossed her legs and swiped at his hand.

"I've seen you around town, haven't I?"

Naturally, it was possible. He had lived in Henley's Edge all his life—thirty-three years. Although he could have been certain he would have remembered seeing someone as beautiful as Gemma.

"I walk in the mornings on Cobble Road sometimes," he said.

"By yourself?"

Ghost nodded.

Gemma motioned to his cellphone. "Why don't you take my number?"

Ghost stammered, unsure. He could scarcely believe it. After he passed his phone into Gemma's hands, her fingers flicked across his screen as she entered her number. Then, when she was finished, she passed it back into Ghost's hands.

"We could walk together sometime," she said.

Ghost sensed himself quiver slightly. The very idea of being alone with Gemma somewhere felt indecent, as if the thought were a corrosive chemical eating away at the memory of his beloved Hailey. Of course, he had occasionally entertained the idea of seeking out new companionship—especially late at night, when rooms in the house felt especially vacant as if they were tombs. Whether his companion was male or female, he was and always would be invisible—invisible to the women he adored because he sometimes preferred men, and indistinguishable to the men he cherished because he was known to adore women. Comfort could be found nowhere. He figured Gemma, too, would abandon him if and when she learned of his dalliances with other men.

It was only a matter of time.

It wasn't long before Piper was delivered by the nurse back to her mother in the waiting room. Gemma exchanged pleasantries with Ghost before leaving, encouraging him to call her the next time he might fancy taking a walk.

Not long after they left, another nurse entered the waiting area and called for Ghost. As he made his way out of the room, he sensed the tiny wraith glued around his neck gorging itself on the hopelessness that had gathered there. Ghost conceded there was so much to eat, and there was hardly a day that went by that his little invisible companion went without feeding.

He'd love to starve it, would love to leave the pathetic creature famished and writhing like an insect pinned inside a Petri dish— shriveled up and withered away like a crop of wheat in a summer drought. But that would mean destroying the tiny parasite, willfully denying it until its very existence was nothing more than a dark smear on the world.

And then, what?

He'd merely be left alone with his sadness, his only remaining company—despair. There were many hardships Ghost could endure, but that was certainly not one of them.

CHAPTER TWO

Those in the town of Henley's Edge that knew Ms. Sylvia Childers and called her a friend were keenly aware of the old woman's aversion to blood.

Such revulsion was the stuff of legend, as many could scarcely forget the moment when the dear woman passed out at the annual July 4th picnic simply because the innards of Mrs. Endicott's strawberry rhubarb pie resembled that of a human artery in full bloom.

"Thank goodness she didn't see the cherry cobbler too," the town's mayor had said as volunteers raced to Ms. Childers' side and shipped her away from the banquet table.

Only a select few were privy to Ms. Childers' reason for detesting the sight of blood so vehemently. Of course, folks in town drew their speculations as they often did with things they didn't adequately understand. Even though she had been born and raised in Henley's Edge, and had raised a child with her late husband, very few could imagine the sheer unpleasantness Ms. Childers' had faced when she was a little girl.

She could hardly ever forget it—how she had undressed one morning to take a hot shower, twisted the faucet, and was immediately sprayed with a geyser of blood as black as car oil. Her father had later discovered that a poor, unsuspecting frog had crawled into the piping and met his untimely demise. Regardless, any explanation on his part had done little to comfort his ten-year-old daughter.

Sixty-years later and she still imagined carrying the coppery scent of frog's blood beneath her generously perfumed skin. That's why when she sliced her palm open on a clay pot in the thrift store kitchen, she expected the worst. Ms. Childers regarded the place where her carpet of skin had thinly separated—a small tear no longer than an inch or so and as bloodless as a tattered piece of papier-mâché. Quizzically studying the small cut on her hand for a moment, she wondered if she had somehow miraculously escaped the sight of her own blood. In fact, she wondered if her prayers in earnest to remove her entire body's blood supply had finally been answered.

Yes, she thought. *Perhaps I've been filled instead with champagne.*

Such a notion was proven to be a mere fable, however, when she pressed down on her open palm and a dark red bubble flowered there—a gruesome reminder.

Ms. Childers didn't recall much after that until she finally came to while lying on the kitchen floor of the church's thrift shop. Her head throbbed, a nearby overturned chair, the reason for her headache. With trembling hands, she stumbled from the floor and braced herself against the rim of the kitchen sink. Her hand pained her; blood smeared across her open palm like dark honey.

She turned on the sink faucet and eased her wounded hand beneath the running water, wincing as she watched ribbons of her blood coil away and disappear like indecent thoughts.

When she was finished cleaning the wound, she rummaged through the cupboard until she located a First Aid kit. Popping the small trunk open, she fished inside and discovered a roll of gauze. As she began to mummify her hand, her eyes wandered to the front page of the Henley's Edge Gazette lying crumpled in the nearby waste bin. The page's headline—POLICE CONTINUE SEARCH FOR MISSING GRANDMOTHER.

Ms. Childers studied the grainy black-and-white photograph of the missing woman pasted beside the article—the old woman's permanently frowning mouth, the lines about her forehead, the liver spots ornamenting her neck. She felt her stomach curl, imagining the poor woman lost and defenseless—perhaps even at the mercy of a sadistic monster.

Yes, she thought. *It must be a monster. What human being would do something so horrible to a helpless old woman?*

Ms. Childers reasoned there were far too many similarities in the recent disappearance to the six others reported in Henley's Edge despite the fact that the bodies had yet to be recovered. All seemed to be without family or loved ones nearby and all seemed to be getting on in age. Because of the new town curfews implemented by the local sheriff's department, Ms. Childers had made arrangements with her daughter who lived in Springfield to call her every evening at eight o'clock and check in. The calls were usually tedious. Not because she detested her daughter, but rather because her daughter had married a man she didn't care for and who had no intention of giving her grandbabies.

Ms. Childers concluded that if anything did happen to her, her daughter's husband wouldn't even bat an eye.

However, that was the least of her worries. After all, she had been entrusted by the thrift shop committee with closing the store by herself today and she knew full well she would never hear the end of it if they found she had been rummaging in the room they had quartered off.

It was then she heard a car horn blare outside in the church parking lot. Stumbling toward the window, she watched as a black Rolls Royce entered her view and swerved into a parking spot beneath a nearby tree.

Idling there for a moment, the car's engine revved sweetly the way a teenage driver might entice a young lady from her home late at night. Ms. Childers squinted, peering out the window, straining to identify the shapeless figure slumped in the driver's seat. The way the car horn had called to her, the way the faceless driver lingered in the front seat before exiting—all seemed like an obvious invitation to her. She sensed the muscles between her thighs clenching, long forgotten sensations of excitement brewing deep within her.

Just then, the car door swung open and a gentleman's glistening patent leather shoe descended from the vehicle. Ms. Childers' eyes followed the gentleman's shapely ankle, outfitted in silk pink socks, further up until she detected neatly pressed black pinstriped pants outfitting what she imagined to be rakishly thin legs and thighs. Finally, the gentleman arrived in full view—an ostentatious ornament when compared with his primitive surroundings. One might have assumed he were the preferred dinner guest of a long-since deceased Russian Tsar given the garishness of his formal attire—expensive-looking black velour gloves for each hand, a satin scarlet waistcoat, an ornate bowtie accented with jewelry.

When the gentleman's face arrived into view, Ms. Childers immediately recognized the old man—Heart Crowley. Though not a frequent visitor of the church or the church's thrift shop, Ms. Childers knew of Mr. Crowley's family—how they were one of the first families to settle in Henley's Edge when the town was first established.

Ms. Childers watched as a brown paper bag of groceries fell out from the car, cans and bottles spilling all over the pavement. She remembered how Mr. Crowley's weekly visits to the local supermarket were a topic of idle conversation in town given the sheer amount of his purchases. For such a small and frail old gentleman, she wondered why he felt the need to purchase so much food. While many speculated he was merely preparing for Armageddon, others pondered if he were hosting weekend dinner parties for his out-of-town friends. Mr. Crowley always kept to himself and never interacted much with the locals in Henley's Edge.

That's why Ms. Childers' face paled when she watched him approach the thrift store on a Wednesday afternoon just before the shop was about to close.

What could he possibly want? she wondered.

After all, Mr. Crowley was never one to participate in purchasing second-hand clothing. Ms. Childers recalled overhearing at the supermarket one afternoon how he has all of his cravats handmade and imported from Italy.

It was then that the old woman remembered how she had repeatedly seen Mr. Crowley in the few days preceding. He had been at the supermarket, searching for a jar of pickled herring while she spoke to a friend from church near the canned beans. Then, she had seen him funneling gas into his car at the gas station while she had hurried into the convenience store for milk. Finally, she had noticed him when he had parked his car outside the library while she was dropping off a handful of overdue books she hadn't finished reading.

It was a silly notion, but she couldn't help but wonder if Mr. Crowley was somehow following her. Despite the fact that she had heard from several of the ladies from church that Mr. Crowley preferred the company of other gentlemen, she pondered the legitimacy of their claims. Especially since he was so handsome and had most likely turned most of them down at one time or another.

Regardless, she had prayed for him.

She had unspooled delicate thoughts of him, cobwebbing them in the corners of her mind for many years now. Although they had never spoken, she had imagined scenarios in which they were better acquainted—tedious conversations detailing the exquisite craftsmanship of his black cummerbund softening to more sensuous talk as the ice in their drinks melted away like their inhibitions. Of course, she had tempered her verve when the thoughts became too indecent and prayed to God for forgiveness.

Ms. Childers conceded that much of her luster was irredeemable given her age; however, it wasn't completely unrealistic for a man as devastatingly handsome and charming as Mr. Crowley to be interested in her.

As the gentleman approached the front door of the small building, Ms. Childers raced into the nearby bathroom and pinched her cheeks for more color. Batting her eyes at her reflection, she smeared a clump of mascara from her eyelashes and hastened back out into the store.

The front door's bell chimed, and Mr. Crowley slipped inside.

Ms. Childers sensed herself slowing, movement suddenly impossible as she gazed upon the immaculately dressed gentleman standing at the threshold. She watched him for a moment as he surveyed the racks of clothing stretching in every direction, his every movement to her a mystery as if he were a rare species long since extinct. She couldn't help but notice the fineness of his skin had been powdered with makeup as if he were appearing in a vaudeville show.

Finally, his eyes settled on her and she felt her heart flutter.

"Cold today," he said, peeling the gloves from his hands. "Isn't it—?"

"Yes. Quite." Ms. Childers lurched forward to greet him but stumbled over the chair she had knocked over. Once the embarrassment was behind her, she continued toward him. "Can I help you find anything?"

As he inched closer toward her, she caught the thin fragrance of pine needles clinging to him as if he had been showered with them. She sensed herself softening at the smell that always reminded her of her father.

"I was told you sell cufflinks," he said, eyes darting around the room. "I'm looking for a pair of sterling silver—an inch in diameter and accented with Brazilian emerald. Do you have that?"

"Oh, I'm sorry, sir," Ms. Childers said, closing her blouse's collar. "We don't have anything like that here. We take donations from the community and I'm afraid we wouldn't know what to do with something so expensive."

"It's a pity. I was told they'd be here," Mr. Crowley insisted.

As he gestured, Ms. Childers couldn't help but notice the small silver cufflinks embellished with green ornamenting the ends of the gentleman's sleeves.

"Like the ones you're wearing?" she asked.

Mr. Crowley glanced down at his cufflinks, stammered as if caught and then composed himself. "Precisely."

"I suppose it's a good thing you already own them," Ms. Childers teased.

Mr. Crowley's face hardened, his eyes fixing on her. "Sometimes owning something doesn't mean it's yours."

He began wandering through the racks of clothing, sifting through the hanging jackets and pants on display.

"I expect you have to have them imported," Ms. Childers said. Anything to fill the uncomfortable silence between them.

"Usually," he explained, occasionally glancing up at her. "My clients expect it of me, after all."

Ms. Childers' ears perked at the word. "Clients? You still work?"

She paled immediately, cursing herself for uttering something so senseless. Ms. Childers hoped Mr. Crowley wasn't the type to take offense to something so insensitive. Why would she think he wouldn't be capable of still working? She supposed her shock came from his invention as being a man of the world.

"Of course, my dear," he said. "My expiration date has yet to arrive."

Ms. Childers bowed her head as if donating to him a wordless apology for her impudence. When she glanced at him again, he was cornering her.

"Have you given thought to where you'll spend eternity, my dear?" he asked.

Ms. Childers softened like melting ice cream. Of course, she had given much thought to the matter. After all, it was the reason she donated so generously to the church and volunteered at the thrift store. She knew very well that her place in heaven's court had already been handsomely purchased.

"My soul you mean?" she asked him with caution as if the very word were something of vulgarity.

"Your soul is a contract between you and the Lord," he explained. "I'm talking about an earthly possession—your body."

With a grand flourish, he drew a pamphlet from his breast pocket and shoved it at Ms. Childers. Her eyes scoured the small leaflet—from the small image of a cemetery flanked by two towering Sycamores to the words in bright yellow bold lettering printed along the top of the page: CARTER RIDGE BURIAL PLOTS.

"You sell places to be interred?"

"Precisely," he said. "I've been representing the kind folks at Carter Ridge for fifteen years now. One of the few places in Connecticut to contain an artesian spring. Water so clean you can drink it. It's nothing short of divine."

"Sounds wonderful," Ms. Childers said, imagining the two of them basking in afternoon sunlight while listening to the hypnotic pulse of free-flowing water pumped from beneath the ground.

"Perhaps I'll have the privilege of showing you sometime," Mr. Crowley said, tipping his hat and inching toward the door.

"You're leaving?" she blurted out. Then cringed as if ashamed of such shamelessness. "I mean—I imagine you have clients to tend to."

Mr. Crowley merely shook his head.

Ms. Childers' face warmed, the hint of a smile thawing somewhere beneath her resolve to invent some meaningless excuse to make him linger just a little while longer.

"I'd love to hear more about your services," she said.

Mr. Crowley glanced out the window at his car. Then, his eyes narrowed at Ms. Childers.

"I can offer something far more luxurious, my dear," he said. "I can take you for a visit."

Ms. Childers' cheeks heated red, every indecent thought she had ever conjured of Mr. Crowley now planting themselves permanently in the bed of her thoughts.

"That's very kind of you," she said. "I don't want to be any trouble."

"It won't be any trouble at all," Mr. Crowley assured her. "I'm in dire need of the company."

Ms. Childers grimaced at the reminder.

She was too, after all.

"You walk here, don't you?" he asked.

Ms. Childers shivered slightly. He somehow knew more than she had ever expected.

"Yes," she murmured, embarrassed. "I don't drive."

"I'll be happy to take you home too," he said.

After she closed the store's register and locked the bags of cash in the safety deposit box in the kitchen's pantry, Ms. Childers shadowed Mr. Crowley outside toward his idling car. Her hand pained her a little, but she couldn't be bothered with something so trivial right now.

To her, his vehicle was a thing of magic—a mystical chariot prepared to ferry them far away to some place truly wondrous.

CHAPTER THREE

After Mr. Crowley had cleared the several bags of groceries from the passenger side, heaving them into the back seat, he gestured for Ms. Childers to take her seat.

She had never cruised in a vehicle so luxurious before and felt out of place, her hands neatly folded in her lap as if fearful she might disturb something. Of course, one of her fondest memories from childhood was motoring around the sprawling Connecticut countryside in her father's Plymouth Gran Fury; however, her father's car was a poor comparison to Mr. Crowley's. In fact, Mr. Crowley seemed to recognize her fascination with his ride, occasionally glancing at her as if grading her infatuation.

"If I had known a salesman could afford such a fashionable ride, I would have told my husband he was in the wrong business," she joked, eyeing him as if hopeful he might reward her with a smile.

He didn't.

Although for a moment Ms. Childers wondered how a salesman with a presumably modest salary could afford such an expensive car, she couldn't be bothered to pursue the thought any further. After all, she nearly had to pinch herself—she was being privately chauffeured by one of the most attractive and sought-after men in the town of Henley's Edge. She could scarcely believe it—a scenario she had invented time and time again had finally come true.

"What does he do?" Mr. Crowley asked.

Ms. Childers stammered, unsure whom he was talking about.

"Your husband," he said, reminding her.

Yes, of course, how could she forget? It was then she realized her husband's memory seemed like nothing more than a shadow of a dim vapor, a dying specter—almost as if something were draining the very thought of him from her mind.

"He died a few years ago," was all the old woman could suddenly recall.

"I'm very sorry," Mr. Crowley said, his brittle voice thinning to a mere whisper.

Ms. Childers stormed her mind for recollections of him— birthdays they had celebrated, holidays they had shared together— and all seemed to quietly shrink from her like perennials that close when you go to touch them. She sensed her face scrunching, parts of her mind withering. It was then she made the horrible realization— she could no longer imagine what he had looked like. It was as if someone had crept into her coils of memory and dragged the thoughts of him screaming by their roots from the bed of her mind.

Mr. Crowley glanced at her, noticing her sudden discomfort.

"Is something wrong?"

Ms. Childers' mouth hung open, as if desperately trying to comprehend. She wondered what else she might forget, what other thoughts might abandon her as suddenly. For the first time, she felt old and, dare she admit it, helpless.

"It's the strangest thing," Ms. Childers said. "I can't seem to remember him. It's—as if my mind had been smeared with black paint."

She felt silly, expecting Mr. Crowley to be thinking the same of her as well. But she couldn't deny what it had felt like—as if a dark curtain had been pulled across her mind's eye, the giant theater of her thoughts lit only by a single gaslight. She couldn't help but wonder if that single light would eventually go out too.

It was then Ms. Childers sensed the car slowing down, Mr. Crowley's foot easing on the brakes, as they rounded a corner near the town's old sawmill and sailed down a tree-flanked gravel lane.

"I hope you don't mind, but I thought we might take the scenic route," Mr. Crowley said.

Of course, Ms. Childers didn't mind. Anything to keep her from returning home to her pathetic one-bedroom apartment where the tap water ran brown and the mice scurried in the walls. Anything else was far more preferable than being left alone with her thoughts—or even worse, the fact that she couldn't remember.

After drifting along a tree-flanked corridor for several minutes, the car made a swift turn and lumbered down a private driveway where the trees were too dangerously close to the sides of the road. It wasn't long before a massive house came into view, dwarfing the neighboring skyline of trees as they were merely children's toy props.

The house was built in the Tudor style, of that Ms. Childers was certain. Although she wouldn't necessarily call herself an expert in such an area, the house's steeply pitched gable roof, extravagantly constructed chimney, and ornamental half-timbering were all blatant indicators of the Tudor style as she well knew. For a moment, she remembered how she and her father would take joyrides on Sunday afternoons and purposely drive around in the more expensive residential communities to spy on the types of houses they inhabited. However, it wasn't long before such a fond memory cracked apart as if made of clay—a giant, invisible hand reaching into her thoughts snatching the very recollection from her.

"I just have to run inside and fetch something," Mr. Crowley explained, parking the car near the house's front entrance.

"This is your home?" Ms. Childers asked, wide eyed and filled with childish wonder at the sight of the monstrosity.

"For five generations," Mr. Crowley said, winking at her before shifting the gear into "park" and exiting the vehicle. "You're welcome to come inside."

Ms. Childers sensed her stomach curling again—the very prospect of being invited into Mr. Crowley's home nearly made her retch. Of course, she had imagined what they might do in private despite her prayers to God in earnest to wipe the indecent thoughts from her. Without warning, she recognized something queer—no matter how desperately she attempted to fling the lewd thoughts from her mind, they seemed to bury themselves deeper in her subconscious. It felt as though someone were begging her to consider such vile things despite her desire to abandon them.

Ms. Childers crawled out of the idling car and followed Mr. Crowley up the front steps and into the foyer. Her head swiveled this way and that as she entered, her eyes darting from expensive-looking furniture, likely imported from the Orient, to the taxidermy heads of wild beasts from exotic expeditions decorating the walls. Perhaps the most outlandish trophy of Mr. Crowley's collection—a giant mural detailing a gruesomely mangled Christ tied to a wooden cross while a massive, faceless shape, lightning blooming from where its head should be, presided over the grisly scene.

It was then she noticed other religious relics decorating the space—iron crucifixes studded with various kinds of expensive jewelry, glass suncatchers hanging from the ceiling and painted with various scenes of holy iconography.

Ms. Childers' breathing slowed until it was a mere whisper. Just then, she noticed Mr. Crowley was staring at her, gleefully taking in her bemusement.

"There's something I have to tell you," he said, approaching her.

She sensed her knees quiver, threatening to give way as he closed in on her.

"Things are quite—different here," he explained.

Then, he commanded her gauze-wrapped hand. She gave it to him without comment, merely watching as he unspooled the dressing. Her hand was stripped bare in a matter of seconds, the small wound pouting at her.

Mr. Crowley pressed down inside the palm of her hand, a dark thread drooling from the small hole there. Ms. Childers swayed back and forth, threatening to collapse. But Mr. Crowley seized her before she could topple, holding her tight in his arms.

"Watch," he said to her.

Then, as he waved his hand over her open palm, she sensed the tear in her hand close as if the edges of her skin had been knitted together. She watched as ropes of blood vanished from her hand, disappearing as if they were merely beads of water beneath a hairdryer.

When the wound had fully closed and the blood had melted away, Ms. Childers' eyes rose and met Mr. Crowley's.

"What are you?" she asked.

Mr. Crowley smiled, as if delighted by the old woman's beguilement. In fact, Ms. Childers wondered if he fed off it—if he were surreptitiously gorging on her bewilderment.

"There's something I want to show you," he said, gliding across the foyer toward the cellar door.

Something deep inside Ms. Childers—a thin wisp of a voice— told her to leave, told her to drag herself kicking and screaming from the house if need be.

But the poor old woman couldn't.

Her entire body suddenly felt as if it were hardening like cooling beeswax. She couldn't move, let alone consider escaping. After all, why would she want to? She pondered what other sublime powers Mr. Crowley must possess, what other enchanting miracles lay dormant inside him. She wondered if he could prevent her from getting any older, if he could somehow primp her wrinkled skin until it was as smooth and creamy as it was when she was a girl. She wondered, though felt silly for even thinking it, if he owned a remedy for grief—if he somehow possessed the cure for the most insufferable malady of all: an old woman's loneliness.

Her feet pulled after him until she flanked him beside the open cellar door. She didn't hesitate, didn't allow her mind to wander since there was nothing left to consider—all had been suddenly vacuumed from her and she realized she was as hollow as a glass lightbulb without even the faintest glow.

Ms. Childers descended the stairs, her memory dimming with

each and every step she took until the very prospect of thought was swept away by a bloodless tide curling at the shores of her empty mind.

It was less than a week later when news first appeared in the Henley's Edge Gazette that Ms. Sylvia Childers had vanished from the local thrift store—a somber-looking black-and-white photograph appearing on the front page of the newspaper just like the others.

CHAPTER FOUR

After meeting with the doctor and explaining the severity of his most recent headaches, Ghost was sent to a neighboring wing of the hospital where they could perform a CT scan. The doctor hadn't seemed troubled, but rather seemed to humor Ghost's nervousness. There was something in the way the doctor had sneered, as if genuinely amused by Ghost's uneasiness.

Ghost reasoned that just as the small spirit tethered to him fed from his worry, there were people who did the same—people with an appetite for hardship or misfortune simply because it let them know that the worst had not yet happened to them. Little reminders that things could be much worse.

Of course, they could be.

But not for Ghost.

Once he had undressed and changed into the hospital gown the nurse had passed to him, Ghost was led into a small room where he was greeted by a doe-eyed twenty-something year old in a white lab coat. He refrained from defining their gender outright because the technician seemed to exist somewhere on the broad spectrum between male and female—a glorious congress of both sexes.

Ghost first noticed the technician's eyes—smeared with crimson and sapphire, colors so garish that only an exotic bird could compare. He couldn't help but observe the plumpness of the technician's lips shining with gloss and surrounded by immaculately groomed dark facial hair. When the technician passed underneath the overhead light, their bald head glowed like the halo of a cherub in an Italian fresco.

"Ready?" the technician asked, steering Ghost toward the machine.

Ghost shivered slightly as the technician's hand curled around his arm. He could scarcely recall the last time he had been touched, let alone acknowledged by someone so unashamedly magnificent. Ghost figured that the technician knew nothing about invisibility, knew nothing about the unbearable ordeal of being left behind by others or deserted because grief is somehow infectious.

He wondered if the technician had ever felt truly alone before— if lonesomeness had ever called upon them in the darkest moments of their despair. Ghost felt strange, eyes avoiding the technician at all costs. He felt as if he were an endangered species, an inheritor of a long since dead language only he seemed to know and only he seemed to be able to speak.

After the technician briefly explained the procedure to him, Ghost leaned his cane against a nearby chair and climbed into the machine—a long tube about the size of an Egyptian sarcophagus. Ghost had seen one on display when he and Hailey had visited the Natural History Museum during a trip to New York City.

As morbid as it was to think at the time, he had once imagined he and Hailey being buried together when the time came—their bodies bound in a permanent embrace the way certain types of creeping plants clung to walls until the unforgiving laws of time shriveled them both to nothing more than dark stains. Now he nearly retched at the thought of Hailey beneath the ground and on her own—the eggs of blow flies bursting from the molten pits where her eyes once were, beetles spilling from between her elastic lips already blackened with blight, earthworms burrowing through the empty socket where her nose once was.

She was not only interred at the Henley's Edge cemetery, but in the graveyard that Ghost had built within his mind as well. He had lovingly composed a giant monument in her honor—a marble statue of her reading, ivy crawling across her as if it were a pashmina. He had visited her there many times, had delivered flowers and other little gifts—anything to ask for forgiveness.

It was his fault she was there, after all.

It was all his fault.

As the CT machine whirred to life and began to scan him, Ghost's mind wandered to the night that had changed his life forever. He never conjured the thought; in fact, it had been coming to him less and less frequently. But, for some reason, it was now a hurricane screaming itself raw directly in his face—the very same storm that had followed his Chevrolet as he and Hailey had meandered home from the supermarket.

Ghost recalled the moment when he had watched the sky turn as emerald as seawater, the air stirring with electricity as if it were an admonition that something was about to happen. Indeed, something was. Ghost would never forget it as long as he lived—how the rain had battered the car windshield as the wipers furiously tossed back and forth, how lightning had sprouted from the darkness as black as iron just outside the ring of light where his car headlights could reach.

"Pull over," Hailey had begged him, rubbing her swollen stomach and the unborn child that had been growing in there for the past eight months.

"We can make it," Ghost had assured her, easing on the gas.

He recalled how the car had sped further down the empty country road, the windshield completely blurred with rain. He winced, remembering how Hailey had begun to breathe more heavily, drawing in labored breaths as if pained. He recalled glancing at her, watching as she had struggled to unbuckle the seat belt tightening about her waist.

"Can you breathe?" Ghost had asked, struggling to help her.

But she hadn't the chance to answer.

Just as Ghost's eyes had jerked back to the road, he saw a pair of approaching headlights sailing toward him. Swerving to avoid the oncoming car, he had twisted the steering wheel and drove the car off the roadway. He recalled how they had glided in the air for a moment, flying as if their vehicle were being carried in the hands of a giant, invisible deity. Without warning, the car had slammed into the base of an oak tree, Hailey's body sailing through the car's windshield as it exploded in a glittering hailstorm.

Ghost sensed his throat tightening, the CT scan cylinder seeming to shrink in around him as if it were a cocoon. He began to convulse, his limbs thrashing the same way they had when paramedics had arrived at the scene and peeled his body from the wreckage.

The technician dragged Ghost out of the machine and hauled him into a chair where he sat, head buried between his knees and cried.

Although he expected he might, Ghost felt no shame for sobbing in front of the technician. Soon this would be a distant memory for them, washed away by a flood of neglect or indifference. Why should anyone care?

After he composed himself, Ghost was returned to the men's changing room where he undressed from the hospital gown. He sat on a bench, naked and sobbing for what felt like hours. When he was finished—almost as if he had somehow plugged the leak behind his eyes—he dressed himself and called the local taxi company to take him home.

As he stepped out from the hospital entrance and onto the sidewalk, he noticed how the autumn air seemed to churn, almost as if it were a sign—a warning, telling him that something else, something far more dreadful, was on its way.

CHAPTER FIVE

Indeed, there was something dreadful on its way—something pernicious and yet invisible as if it were some infectious disease knitting a grotesque patchwork of a suffering humanity. Regrettably, this was no mere malady, no feverish sickness to be cured by a mere antibiotic.

Sergeant Nadeem Malik knew this as he stood on his front lawn in the early hours of the morning when the street lights began to dim and the peril of more misfortune whisked through town like the specter of an errant locomotive—an otherworldly machine sent to capture another poor, unsuspecting resident of Henley's Edge and spirit them far away.

Ms. Sylvia Childers had been the fifth disappearance in as many months and Malik couldn't shake the agonizing feeling that more were to come, the autumn wind blowing all around him with a threat—an invocation of terrible things to be conjured, of misery and anguish to flood the helpless town in water as black and as thick as molasses until they all had slipped beneath the surface and drowned.

Yes, he thought to himself. *Perhaps that's where we'll find her: in the town river, her bloated body swaddled in a cradle of thin reeds.*

He hoped he'd be wrong, that there was some chance she and the others were still out there and waiting to be rescued. After all, the police department had already scoured nearly every inch of wetlands and forest in the province and hadn't turned up so much as an earring, let alone a missing body. The strangest thing about those who had disappeared—all were in their sixties and seventies, and many of them didn't have cellphones. Malik reasoned this was perhaps why they were being targeted—easy to abduct and even easier to wipe all trace of them from the world.

He thought of people like his grandparents, now long dead—the people who had raised him, taught him what it meant to be a Muslim man, from a little boy when his parents had both died at the age of eighteen. He flinched, thinking of those who had encouraged him to put them away in a home when their minds had begun to deteriorate like the face of a coin abandoned in a riverbed. To most, the elderly were burdens—pruned wraiths of days long since passed, inhuman creatures to be warehoused and then forgotten about. After all, Malik admitted, many were quick to refuse souvenirs of mortality, living embodiments of what's to come.

As he sipped his morning coffee, he winced when he imagined the poor old men and women that had been taken—he thought of them frightened and helpless, knees buckling and urine running down from between their legs as they shivered like lost children somewhere probably dark and cold.

What kind of monster would do something like this? he wondered.

Just then, his husband, Brett, appeared beside him and startled him with a plate of burnt toast.

"I thought you might be hungry," he said, shoving the plate at Malik.

Malik forced a half-hearted smile, eyeing the burned slices of bread. "Burned again?"

"I'm blaming the toaster," Brett contested playfully. "I'm thinking of going down to the bank and opening a new account just to get a new one. They're running a special this month."

Out of his peripheral vision, Malik noticed a thin figure dashing down the lane in front of their house. When he turned to look, he recognized it as their neighbor—a sixty-year-old retired accountant named Mr. Reiling dressed in a bright neon colored track suit. Malik raised his hand to wave as he made eye contact with the old gentleman, but Mr. Reiling seemed troubled—eyes avoiding Malik and his husband at all costs as he sprinted down the road faster until finally disappearing as if to escape their sight.

Malik glanced down and it was then he noticed he and Brett's hands were bound together—a common display of affection for some, and yet a vile monstrosity when the hands belonged to two men. They pulled apart, eyes lowering as if embarrassed, as if suddenly remembering they should be ashamed.

Malik had been taught that shame.

They both had.

It had been nearly seven months since they had first moved into the small Dutch Colonial at the end of Elizabeth Street and not a single neighbor had visited to introduce themselves.

Though, that's not to say that their neighbors weren't immediately suspicious of the young men that had moved in as they had made their uneasiness apparent in no uncertain terms. Malik would often go to the kitchen window in the morning or early evening and notice several of the neighbors slowing to a crawl in front of their house, cautiously peering inside as if Malik and his husband were rare exotic animals imported from faraway lands, never-before-seen species captured from another world and delivered to earth for research.

It hadn't been long before their home began to feel like a fishbowl, as if they were extinct specimens dredged from the bottom of the sea, dumped into a tank and forced to entertain the masses. If you could even call it entertainment, that is. To Malik, the looks he and his husband received from neighbors were as if he had stolen a newborn, cut off its ears, and sprinkled the shrieking infant with gasoline before lighting a match.

"Don't forget we have a Zoom meeting with the adoption counselor later tonight," Brett reminded him as they steered back into the house's foyer.

Although he loathed to admit it, the very last thing on Malik's mind was the adoption—the precious child Brett had dreamed of since the day they had first met. More than anything, Brett wanted to be a father. But, for Malik, the drive simply wasn't there. It's not that he opposed the idea of fathering a child, especially with a partner as loving and as gentle as Brett. He was merely afraid of somehow hurting the poor thing, somehow damaging the child beyond repair just as he had been when he was younger.

"I might be late tonight," Malik said, adjusting his tie in the antique mirror beside the front doorway. "Can you manage without me?"

Malik noticed how Brett's shoulders seemed to drop, his head lowering.

"I hope this won't be a regular thing," Brett said.

Of course, Malik recognized he had been absent for much of the past five months, and if Brett weren't such an understanding husband, Malik might have been tossed away like a rain-soaked newspaper. But, thankfully, Brett wasn't like that. Brett was kind and comforting, qualities from which Malik could certainly learn. Brett was everything a father should be, even if Malik knew he could never compare.

Malik pulled his husband close to him, cupping the left side of his face.

"Look," he said to him, "I'll promise to be there—when the time comes."

Although Brett probably thought Malik was stalling once more as was his custom, Malik had every intention of being the father Brett desired him to be.

But, luckily, that day was not today.

The first thing Malik seemed to notice about Ms. Sylvia Childers' daughter, Lillian, was how out of place the thirty-something year old woman seemed when in her mother's apartment—an uninvited guest, as if she were fearful of upsetting the delicate balance her mother had left in her absence. Lillian carefully maneuvered about the clutter in the small one-bedroom residence as if balancing on a tightrope, her every movement being graded, delivering a tray of tea to the living room where Malik was waiting.

"You had an arrangement with your mother to speak on the phone every evening?" Malik asked, referring to his small notepad. "When did that start?"

"Yes," Lillian answered after she finished pouring the tea, sitting on the divan across from Malik. "I guess it started back in the summer when the first two went missing. I was worried."

Malik couldn't help but notice how Lillian would occasionally push the tip of her index finger in her mouth, chewing on her nail until it was a mere blistered nub—a nervous habit inherited from grade school, he imagined.

"And the last time you spoke with your mother was the night before you reported her missing?" he asked.

"That's correct," Lillian said, pouring him a piping hot cup of tea and ladling two small sugar cubes into the cup. "She missed our usual eight o'clock call and I knew something was wrong. You know that feeling you get when you know something's off?"

Of course, Malik knew the feeling. He had felt the same sensation any time he would go out in public with Brett, as if their handholding or their pecks on the cheeks were abominations, despicable perversions to be reviled or gawked at.

"So, I called one of her neighbors to check the apartment and she wasn't here," Lillian explained.

Malik's eyes wandered to the walnut credenza beside the apartment entrance where he noticed a marble miniature statue of Christ being held in the arms of his mother as if it were an homage to Michelangelo's *La Pietà*. His eyes drifted further up the wall and it was there he noticed a wrought iron crucifix beside the doorway—a small figurine of Christ pinned to the object and staring down at him like a disapproving schoolmaster.

"She doesn't have a cellphone, correct?" Malik asked. "Otherwise, we would've already traced it."

Lillian shook her head. "I kept telling her to get one. I told her that the next time I visited we'd go to the mall and pick one out together."

Malik leaned forward in his chair, eyeing Lillian in such a way that told her he would help her only if she complied, only if she told the truth. "Is there anything else you can remember that she might have said the night you spoke to her last? Anything you may have forgotten."

"I told the police everything."

"Maybe something that didn't seem important at the time," Malik said.

Lillian thought for a moment, pushing her index finger between her front teeth and chewing there as her mind raced.

"She told me she was volunteering at the church thrift shop from noon until when they close," she said. "My mom was excited because she had put a pair of pants she had wanted on layaway, and she could finally afford them."

"We have those pants in a bag down at the station," Malik said, referring to his notes. "Wherever she went, she didn't take them with her."

Lillian dropped her head between her knees, coming to terms with the fact that her mother may never return—that something had been done that was quite irreversible. The thought seemed to swallow her completely until she curled up in a ball the way small pill bugs do when you poke at them.

"Oh, God," she heaved, panting.

"Is there anything else you can think of?"

Lillian composed herself, straightening herself the way Malik imagined Victorian schoolgirls might when balancing a stack of books on their heads.

"I suppose… It's hardly worth mentioning."

Malik leaned forward in his seat. "Yes?"

Lillian strained an uncomfortable smile, as if not quite believing the absurdity of what she was about to say. "My mother was—quite enamored with a particular gentleman in town," she said. "She was delighted because he seemed to be appearing wherever she went."

"Did she tell you a name?"

"She never would," Lillian said. "My mother thought talking about those kinds of things was—inappropriate. I was surprised she told me in the first place."

Malik considered this for a moment. "So, there was someone she was smitten with?"

"Someone she admired, I guess," Lillian answered.

"That's very helpful, Mrs. Jones," Malik said, making a small note in his notepad and closing it.

He rose from his seat and made his way to the front door, Lillian following close behind.

"You'll let me know if you hear anything?" she asked, nervously wringing her hands.

"Of course," he assured her. "You'll be staying in town for a while?"

"I got a room at the motel in Litchfield," she said. "I couldn't bear to stay here on my own. Not with what's going on."

Malik couldn't blame the poor woman. Even the most devout clergyman might find Ms. Childers' use of décor too enthusiastic, too ridiculously excessive—holy relics lining the walls and the mantles.

"I'll be in touch," he said, glancing at the small figurine of Christ beside the door glaring at him. He winced slightly, the figurine's glass eyes seeming to follow him wherever he moved.

Returning to his car parked in front of the affordable housing complex, he hung his head and took a deep breath. He had missed afternoon prayer as usual but promised himself he would make it up later that night. As he stood beside his car and thought—thought of Ms. Childers, thought of the Christ figurine pinned to the wall, thought of anything—there was positively no way Malik could have known that Ms. Childers' abductor was freely prowling the nearby streets and already eyeing his next victim.

CHAPTER SIX

It was later than usual when Malik finally returned home, pulling his car into the garage and lowering the bay door. He half-expected Brett to be waiting for him with a stern lecture, an admonition of others who had let relationships wither and die because their career demanded too much of them—a recital he had heard time and time again. Or perhaps, even worse, Brett would already be in bed—curled up in the corner and deathly quiet like a lovesick schoolboy.

Surprisingly, there was no sign of him when Malik first came into the house—no portent of a grim discourse to be recited, hardly any evidence of a warm dinner now wasted.

"Brett?" he called out, switching on the living room lamp and scanning the empty room.

It was then he heard the faintest murmur of music drifting down from the upstairs bathroom. When he came to the door, pushing it open, he found Brett naked and reclining in the bubble-filled bathtub with a glass of red wine in his hand and a satin blue sleep mask covering his eyes. The mask was accented with a golden trim and decorated with the over exaggerated eyelashes of a drag queen—a cover so over the top that only Holly Golightly might have found it fashionable. In fact, Brett often jokingly referred to the mask as "Holly" whenever he wore it.

"Darling," Malik exhaled, delighted by the sight.

Brett stirred, lifting his mask and glaring at Malik. He leaned out of the tub and twisted the radio's volume until the music hushed to a mere whisper.

"Holly looks beautiful tonight," Malik said, gesturing to the mask as Brett discarded it beside the tub.

Brett said nothing.

Malik dragged a chair from beside the wall and propped it near the bathtub.

"You're mad," he said, lowering his head. "I know."

Brett twisted the glass in his hand, wine as dark as blood swirling there. "I was mad three hours ago."

"And now?"

Brett exhaled and downed another gulp. "Now I'm just drunk."

"I told you it might go longer than usual tonight," Malik said, dipping his hand beneath the bath water and pushing a cloud of bubbles toward his husband.

"Dinner's burned," Brett said, folding his arms and sinking further into the water. "I hope you didn't want any."

"We could order takeout," Malik reminded him.

But Brett wasn't appeased, his eyes seeming to avoid Malik at all costs—not because he was upset, but rather because he seemed to know his playful anger might weaken if he stared at his husband long enough.

"Please don't be mad," Malik begged him, rubbing Brett's fingers as they gripped the rim of the bathtub.

Malik knew exactly how to thaw Brett's resolve. He leaned in close and pecked him on the forehead. At once, Brett seemed to melt, his guard lowering as he uncrossed his arms. Finally, Brett's eyes found Malik's—they were wide and wonder-filled, the same way English settlers might have gazed upon a virgin forest. Malik was only too eager to be claimed.

"Join me?" Brett said, spreading his legs to make room.

Malik didn't hesitate, undressing and climbing into the tub until the mountain of bubbles had swallowed him up.

"So, you had a good day?" Brett asked, twisting the dial on the radio.

"No. Not really," Malik said, slumping down further beneath the water. "I can't seem to catch a break."

"You will."

But Malik wasn't convinced. "I just feel like I'm letting people down."

"You're not letting anyone down," Brett said, gently rubbing Malik's hands.

"I've been thinking of my grandparents a lot lately," Malik said, his eyes drifting off. "I can't seem to shake them."

"Why would you want to? I know how close you were with them."

Malik smiled at the memory. "They took care of me better than my parents could." His voice firming, he added, "I'm glad they're not around."

"Why?"

Malik shook his head. "I don't know what I would have done if something horrible had happened to them."

"There's not another reason you're glad they're not here anymore, is there?" Brett asked, leaning closer toward him.

"What?"

Brett grabbed a nearby washcloth and sponged his forehead. "You never had to tell them about us."

"That's different."

"Is it?"

"I would've told them eventually," Malik assured him.

"You think they still would've loved you?"

Of course, it was a question Malik had considered time and time again—would his grandparents have still cared for him if they had known of his sexual preferences? Although he was resolute in his belief that their love would have never changed, there was a small, quiet voice whispering to him that it might have changed everything.

"They told me that their love for me would never change," Malik said, his voice trembling slightly as if not fully convinced. "No matter what."

"You know that for sure?" Brett asked.

"It's what I choose to believe."

Just then, their ears perked at the sound of glass shattering downstairs followed by the shrill screech of tires against pavement outside.

"What was that?" Brett asked, turning off the radio and swiping a nearby towel.

"Stay here," Malik said, climbing out of the bathtub and wrapping a towel around his waist.

Creeping down the stairs, Malik came into the living room and switched on the lights. His eyes darted to the windows overlooking the small rose garden Brett had arranged in the front of the house. He saw the curtains billowing like the gowns of lovelorn specters, a giant, gaping hole in one of the bay windows. As his eyes travelled across the room, it wasn't long before he found a large red brick tied with a small note lying in the center of the living room rug.

"Darling?" Brett called to him from the top of the stairwell.

"Stay there, babe. Don't come down here," he ordered.

Malik snatched the brick from the ground and tore the string off, uncrumpling the note. He sensed something whisper deep inside him—as if an invisible hand had reached inside his chest and squeezed him until he could no longer breathe. His watering eyes ran over the two words scrawled on the piece of paper in childlike lettering—two words that had struck him like a whaler's harpoon as if he were nothing more than a loathsome beast to be caught and sold at auction.

The two words that had changed his life forever, two words that every gay man knew and feared deeply in his heart—DIE FAGGOTS.

After the police had arrived and surveyed the area, they took Malik and Brett to separate areas in the house for questioning. Malik sat at the kitchen table, his eyes staring blankly at the note as one of the officers bagged it for evidence.

"You didn't hear anything else?" Captain Chisholm asked Malik, circling him.

"Just the sound of the window breaking and the tires screeching."

"You didn't see anyone? Anything?" the Captain asked.

Malik shook his head. There hadn't been anything else. Or had there? Had he misremembered? Had he blocked something out to spare his beloved husband? He felt stupid, as if he should have been expecting something like this to happen, as if he should have somehow expected something far crueler.

"We'll ask around the neighbors," Captain Chisholm said. "See if they saw anything unusual tonight."

Malik remained silent. He knew it would be a waste of time. None of them would talk to the Captain, let alone invite him in their homes. After all, for all he knew, one of them had sent the brick flying through their window—a thoughtful housewarming gift they had always intended to deliver. Malik couldn't help but wonder if the lot of them had pooled their resources to execute the endeavor—an admonition that the worst was yet to come.

"Collins, head outside for a moment, would you?" the Captain ordered the young Officer bagging evidence.

After he had left, Captain Chisholm pulled a chair out from the table and sat across from Malik.

"You know we'll do what we can, but there's no guarantee we'll find them," he said. "Not without an eyewitness report."

Malik searched his mind, straining to recall something he might have seen when driving home earlier in the evening—a sign, a warning, anything.

Nothing came to him.

He thought of the neighbors, slowing as they walked by in the early morning or in the late evening—their prying eyes, their glances filled with disdain.

Malik shook his head, his shoulders dropping. "The neighbors won't talk to you."

"You think it was one of them?" the Captain asked, leaning forward in his seat.

Of course, it was one of the first things Malik had thought of when he first read the note. But he couldn't be certain.

"I don't know," he said.

Malik watched Captain Chisholm draw a deep breath, as if sensibly combing the corners of his mind for the proper words to say.

"You know, there is the possibility that you and your—husband— brought this on yourselves," he said.

Malik could scarcely believe his ears. Had the Captain really just said that? He felt sick, his stomach performing the somersaults of an Olympic gymnast.

Not this, he thought to himself. *Anything but this.*

"I've watched the way you behave in public," the Captain began. "Of course, it's your business. But holding hands and kisses on the cheek—it's not how I'd expect you to act."

Malik glared at him. "How exactly do you expect me to act?"

The Captain rose from his seat and began pacing the kitchen in front of Malik. "My wife has a beautiful diamond necklace that I bought for her on vacation in Greece. It's one of a kind. Very expensive. Very rare. I never let her wear it outside the house. Do you know why? It would attract the wrong attention."

The Captain paused, as if hopeful Malik might say something. He didn't.

"I think something like this could have been easily prevented if you and your..." he said, his voice beginning to trail off. "If you both were more discreet. Remember, a little goes a long way."

The Captain patted Malik on the shoulder the same way an adult might belittle a child. Then, he pushed the chair underneath the table and ambled out of the room to leave Malik alone with his thoughts, abandoning him the way napalm-scented civilians would single-file march from their burning homelands, forming a glorious diaspora.

With or without discretion, Malik couldn't shake the horrible feeling that someone was out there—delighting in their agony, worshipping their distress, and wishing them far worse. He gazed out the kitchen window and couldn't bear the thought of the darkness sprouting eyes and staring back at him and Brett—other visitors waiting to call upon them with far more vile offerings.

He thought of promises made to his husband, passions squeezed to the size of a child's hand glove and folded neatly into a pocket to be long forgotten—a livid current of whitewater approaching and threatening to drag everything he ever loved out toward the infinite deep where it would never be seen again.

CHAPTER SEVEN

I t was early in the evening when the taxicab pulled onto the shoulder of the road in front of Ghost's house, idling there as he crawled from the backseat with his brown paper bag of groceries. After tipping the driver, Ghost ambled up the stone pathway leading to the front door. Of course, he always took his time when walking since it often pained him; however, he always found himself slowing to a crawl when approaching his home in the evening—anything to spare him the unbearable silence that waited for him in his now permanently empty abode.

He'd turn on the TV and crank the volume up loud to make it seem as though others were nearby—guests he would pretend were milling about in another room—but it was hardly comforting. Perhaps the most unbearable reminder of his lonesomeness—climbing into a bed built for two. That was why he preferred sleeping on the couch despite the displeasure of his chiropractor.

Glancing up as he limped, Ghost noticed a peculiar looking gentleman dressed in a pinstriped suit three sizes too big and guarding the house. The man was perhaps no older than fifty but appeared much older, resembling a well-dressed gentleman in a classic Hollywood production—neatly shined crocodile loafers on both feet and a black top hat to hide his thinning nest of hair.

"Mr. Everling?" the gentleman called out, approaching.

Ghost immediately shrank from him, cautious. "Yes."

"I'm Gerald Pinner of Marsh Credit Collection Services in Waterbury," he said, plucking a small business card from his breast pocket and passing it to Ghost. "Here's my card."

Ghost studied the card for a moment. Of course, he had been expecting this. He stupidly hadn't planned an escape in case it happened.

"Right now isn't the best time," he said, swerving around Mr. Pinner and fumbling in his coat pocket for his house keys.

"This won't take long," Mr. Pinner promised him.

After unlocking the door and stepping inside, Mr. Pinner followed Ghost.

"I assume this is about the—"

Ghost could hardly say it, the words like a stem of ragweed burning in his throat which the tiny spirit had shoved there.

"The thousands of dollars that have remained unpaid for nearly eight months now," Mr. Pinner reminded him.

"Yes, that."

"Precisely eleven thousand three hundred seventy-four dollars and eighty-nine cents," Mr. Pinner said, referring to a small notebook from his pocket.

Ghost's eyes drifted to the cane in his right hand. He thought of the doctor that had told him he might never walk again without expensive therapy.

"Some bills came up," Ghost said, reminded of the pain in his hip—the agony that showed no signs of abandoning him even though everything else seemed eager to. "I didn't really have a choice."

"We are understanding up to a certain point," Mr. Pinner explained, referring to his notebook again. "We've sent eight letters in the mail, have tried to make contact over the phone almost ten times, have left six voice messages."

Ghost felt himself shriveling, as if his limbs were suddenly made of elastic. "I was planning to make a payment next week."

"Mr. Everling, we've sent numerous letters requesting payment," Mr. Pinner said, his voice firming. "Personal contact, like this, is the final step before more drastic measures are taken."

Ghost recoiled until he was pressed against the wall. "I have every intention of making a payment. I just—need another week."

Mr. Pinner straightened, as if he had been prepared for Ghost's bargaining. "I'm afraid the firm I work for has made it clear, in no uncertain terms, that I'm not to leave your residence without some form of payment today."

Ghost sensed warmth returning to his cheeks. "I told you. I just need more time."

"Perhaps you'd like to accompany me and explain your situation to my superiors?" Mr. Pinner flashed teeth so brownish yellow that his mouth resembled a rusted gate.

Ghost knew for certain he wouldn't escape this. For once, he had a visitor in his home, and it was someone he couldn't wait to be rid of.

"How much will be enough?" he asked, pulling open the credenza drawer and locating his checkbook.

"Dealer's choice."

After he wrote out the check, he passed the small slip to Mr. Pinner.

"Very good," the gentleman said. He turned, about to leave.

Then, turned back to face Ghost. "Of course, you understand that if this check bounces, I'll have the pleasure of seeing you again."

Ghost knew that was true. What's more, he knew for certain the check would bounce. Before another moment of hesitation, he snatched the check from Mr. Pinner's grasp and tore it to shreds. Then, he fished in his pocket for the few twenty dollar bills he had remaining in his wallet—the rest of the money he had for the week.

He passed the cash to Mr. Pinner. "Take this instead," he said.

Mr. Pinner pocketed the money without thanks, heading for the front door. "A pleasure, Mr. Everling. We'll be expecting another payment in a month. Understand?"

Ghost merely nodded like a sniveling child who had soiled fresh underwear in front of the whole classroom.

After Mr. Pinner had left, Ghost stood in the house's entryway like a fanged creature that required invitation to be allowed further inside. He felt invisible, even to himself. As he toured the empty rooms in his house, he scoured the place for things he could sell—little trinkets he could bear to part with and pawn away at the local shop downtown. Everything reminded him of her—the antique silver hairbrush on the nightstand they had picked up on a trip to Vermont, the cast iron teapot they had been gifted by the hotel where they had stayed during their honeymoon in Italy.

Ghost came to the place in the house where his misery seemed to root itself—the nursery on the third floor. The walls were accented with pink and ivory colored vinyl wallpaper, tiny flecks of silver ribboning throughout. In the center of the space was a small cradle, a child's mobile hanging above and dangling with plush toy versions of various farm livestock.

Ghost picked up the small toy lamb he had bought the day before the accident—the toy his child would never play with. He squeezed it tight and then tossed it aside.

His eyes snapped to the nearby wall and noticed the tiny wooden crucifix his wife had once hung there. Beside the cross and positioned on a lower shelf was a handmade needlepoint canvas with "This home is filled with love" stitched into it in exquisite cursive lettering. Ghost swiped the canvas from the shelf and tossed it across the room where it slammed into the radiator, its wooden frame cracking in half with a vulgar crunch like the noise of a bird's wing being snapped in half.

His eyes narrowed at the cross.

Snatching the crucifix from the wall, his thoughts turned to God.

Although Ghost had thought of God many times before, this time he imagined him as a man—a scrawny, pathetic one without clothing and shivering before him like a prisoner awaiting the disgrace of public execution. Ghost thought of peeling the skin from God—carefully unspooling the constellations from His muscle, the shimmering teeth of distant stars and moons from His tissue. He thought of how God might beg him or plead with him.

He had hoped that He would.

Ghost snapped the cross in his hands as if it were made of kindling. Then, he tossed the remains on the floor where the little broken bits scattered like the torn beads from a rosary.

He thought of God lying there—broken, helpless, damaged goods to no longer be worshipped, an unfit thing to be revered.

That was how Ghost had always wanted to think of Him, splitting Him open until God was nothing more than the wind-battered straw remains of a mere scarecrow pulled apart by a passing summer storm.

PART TWO

HE SENT DARKNESS
AND MADE THE LAND DARK

"Those who can make you believe absurdities, can make you commit atrocities."

—Voltaire

CHAPTER EIGHT

There was little that could be done to ease Malik's mind, although Brett did his best to try. Every little tremor their old house made sent the poor man into a panic, every unfamiliar face that passed by the house—a trespasser capable of the most heinous insurrection. Malik took to popping a few pain relievers before bed every night, another stress headache to be nursed when he awoke in the morning. Very little softened the edges digging into him. He seemed to dwell in a permanent state of anxiety, as if there was the horrible possibility that everything could be taken away from him at any moment.

Of course, Brett did his best to comfort his husband—massaging him when he returned home from work or cooking dinner despite his lackluster skillset as a chef. Regardless, Malik could not be consoled. He wouldn't be able to sleep until those who had sent the brick through the window with the note—the warning—were held accountable for their terrorism.

Even a polite knock at the front door on a Saturday afternoon sent his heart quivering. Although Brett was already halfway to the door, Malik begged him not to answer it and went in his place. Peering through the glass, he was greeted by a somber-faced Captain Chisholm. Of course, he thought it was odd. Captain Chisholm never contacted him on weekends, much less made a house visit.

"I hope this isn't a bad time," the Captain said as Malik opened the door.

Malik studied him. Captain Chisholm was an imposing figure—shoulders as broad as the antlers of a young buck, a mustache so well-coiffed he resembled a Parisian gentleman in a painting by Georges Seurat. He kept himself healthy and trim, the regimen of the star athlete of the high school football team still very much a part of his daily routine despite the extra pounds middle age seems to add to a person.

"Something's happened?" Malik asked, eyes widening with the most foolish thing of all—hope. "You've caught them?"

"Not quite."

Captain Chisholm scraped his boots on the "Welcome" mat and pushed inside the house until he was at the threshold of the living room.

"Care for some tea, Captain?" Brett asked. "I can throw a pot on the stove in no time."

"No, thank you," the Captain said, touring the room until he settled on an armchair in the corner. "I won't be long."

As the Captain made himself comfortable, Malik couldn't help but squirm when he recognized how at ease the Captain seemed to be in their home—as if it were a public place, as if the house possessed all the informality of a park where people could come and go as they pleased. Malik loathed the idea of the Captain luxuriating in such unearned comfort in the sanctity of their home. After all, Malik and Brett had quite literally begged, borrowed, and stolen to purchase a home in Henley's Edge. That's exactly what it was always intended to be—a home. It had been their refuge, their sanctuary. It was none of those things any longer, and Malik detested to admit that miserable fact—holding a small funeral for their comfort and safety in the privacy of his mind.

"Something to eat maybe?" Brett suggested. "We have some crackers and brie we haven't opened yet."

"Very kind of you, but I promise this won't take long," the Captain said, brandishing a large folder from beneath his coat. "There's something I wanted to show the both of you."

Malik and Brett sat in the loveseat across from where Captain Chisholm had seated himself. Just as they sat down, Brett reached for Malik's hand and interlocked their fingers the way young lovers do. Malik glanced down, noticing his fingers wrapped around Brett's. As his eyes flashed to the Captain, he noticed Captain Chisholm glaring at their hand holding with visible disdain—as if they were no better than a filthy dish rag, as if they possessed the same perversity of an upside-down cross or a holy text smeared with excrement.

"Something about our case?" Brett asked, oblivious to the Captain's staring.

Malik hated to admit it, but he suddenly felt dirty holding his husband's hand, as if it were undoing him until he was left to merely ravels of skin.

"One of your neighbors kindly supplied us with footage from their street-facing security cameras," the Captain explained, sliding the folder across the coffee table toward them.

Seizing the opportunity to weasel out from his husband's grasp, Malik pulled their hands apart and opened the folder. He was greeted with an enlarged grainy snapshot of the street in front of their house, the blurred outline of a red Subaru with tinted windows sailing down the lane.

"Do you recognize that vehicle?" the Captain asked, leaning forward in his chair. "Maybe a car you've seen driving around the neighborhood at odd hours?"

"Brett would know better than me," Malik said as he titled the photograph toward his husband. "He's home for most of the day."

Brett's eyes went over the photograph again and again. Nothing. He shook his head, deflating.

"Doesn't look familiar to me."

"You have this picture, though," Malik said, hopeful. "That means you have a license plate you can run?"

The Captain closed the folder, snatching it from the table and pocketing it. "Unfortunately, no. The camera didn't record a license plate. But we have the model type and color, which is a start."

"What about keeping an Officer on guard for a week or so?" Malik asked, embarrassed to admit his fear.

"I don't think you have to worry about something like this happening again," the Captain assured them. "Matters like these are usually isolated incidents."

But Malik wouldn't back down. "You won't even entertain the idea?"

"There's no need," Captain Chisholm said. "Certain public behaviors are going to be corrected. Isn't that right?"

He stared down Malik, eyes scouring him for an answer—the answer he had wanted, not the answer Malik was willing to give.

Malik finally gave in.

"Yes," he said. "Things will be—adjusted."

"Very good," the Captain said, smiling and rising from his seat. "I certainly don't mean to keep you. I'll show myself out."

Before Malik or Brett could show him to the door, the Captain was already on his way out and down the front pathway toward his car. After they watched him peel out of their driveway, they closed the door and ambled back to the kitchen like melancholy funeral guests in an unfamiliar home they had just inherited.

"What did he mean by things being corrected?" Brett asked him.

There it was—the question Malik had been dreading since the Captain first said it. He shrank from his husband—rehearsing the proper words in his mind, inventing euphemisms, anything to soften the disappointment.

"It's nothing," Malik said, pushing the empty tea kettle under the sink faucet and filling it up. "Nothing I wanted to trouble you about."

"Something I've done?"

Malik couldn't bear it any longer—the thought of Brett feeling guilty for something that was never his fault, the idea that there were some in this world who would poison others' joy simply for the sheer gratification of it.

"No, nothing you've done," Malik assured him. "It's just—the Captain wants us to keep things less visible. He thinks we should try to—blend in more."

Brett's face scrunched, bewildered. "I thought we were doing fine. I added flannel to my wardrobe for Christ's sake."

Malik patted his husband's cheek, doing his best to comfort him. "This town—this place isn't for people like us. We just have to accept that."

"Can you?" Brett asked.

For once, Brett looked fearful—as if he had received a grim premonition, as if he were a spectator at his own death at the hands of queer-hating hooligans.

Malik wiped the hair from Brett's face, sliding his finger down his rosy cheek. "We just have to try a little harder to fit in, babe," he whispered. "Don't worry. We'll be fine."

Brett softened for an instant before his eyes snapped back to Malik.

"You don't think they'll come back?"

Malik wrapped an arm around him, holding him tight until their bodies were pressed together. "They're going to wish they hadn't if they do."

"Be serious," Brett pleaded with him. "You don't think they'll come back?"

Malik said nothing. How was he to know? After all, he lived in permanent fear of the moment when they would return and finish what they had intended. Although he didn't know for certain if they would come back, but he had been living day to day as if they would. He hated the idea of lying to Brett, consoling him with insincere comfort. But he didn't want to scare him. More importantly, he didn't want to lose him to the same fear eating away at him like a scarab beetle.

"No, they won't come back, babe," Malik assured him. "I promise."

Just as their lips were about to meet, Malik pulled himself away as if remembering his promise to the Captain, as if his every action were being graded even in the privacy of his own house. Brett paled at his husband's shrinking but seemed to quietly understand as he lowered his head and moved away from him. For the remainder of the evening they avoided one another as if they were mythical beasts that would turn on one another and transform the other to a pillar of salt, as if they were rare creatures that would burst into flames upon the slightest touch.

CHAPTER NINE

To Gemma, Mr. Crowley resembled a rare bird—a peculiar animal captured in the Himalaya Mountains or winging over the Adriatic Sea and spearing surface-dwelling fish. As he stood there on her front porch, she couldn't help but steal a moment to regard his exceptionally long fingernails, the length of a hawk's talons and presumably just as sharp. Even the way he dressed conjured the likeness of a bird—the pink velour high waisted pants, the green waistcoat decorated with sequins and jewelry, the top hat accented with different colored feathers. Every aspect of his character seemed like a bid for attention, an invocation of a strange ritual where he was considered God and all others were mere slaves to his most indecent whims.

"You're Ms. Ainsley—?" he said, squinting as he referred to a small note card.

"I'm not interested," she said, threatening to close the door.

But Mr. Crowley was one step ahead of her, sliding his foot across the threshold to wedge the door open further.

"Ms. Carlisle?" he said, referring to his notes again.

Gemma paused, as if the name owned her somehow, as if she owed some invisible debt to the strange man. "Yes?"

"My office was notified you requested more information regarding our reasonably priced burial plots at Carter Ridge," Mr. Crowley explained, pushing a brochure in her face.

Gemma shrank from him, unsure. "Burial plots? I never made a request for that."

Mr. Crowley sighed, flashing the notecard at her with her name and address scrawled on it. "There's no other way I could have this information if you didn't make a request, my dear."

"I'm sure I never made a request for burial plots," she insisted, folding her arms as if it were her only defense. "I think you must be mistaken."

Mr. Crowley seemed to deflate, removing his patent leather shoe from the threshold and retreating to the porch. "It's a pity because I came all this way. My superior isn't going to be pleased. He's not as understanding as I might hope."

Gemma stammered, unsure what to say. "I'm—sorry."

Just as she began to close the door again, Mr. Crowley pivoted and lurched toward her.

"I don't suppose you have a first aid kit nearby. I seem to have sliced my hand open," he said, suddenly revealing his right hand and showing her the blood as it drooled from the small wound in the center of his palm.

Gemma reeled at the sight of the old man's injured hand. "How did that happen? What did you cut it on?"

She couldn't believe her eyes. She didn't see him touch anything sharp in the few seconds he had turned from her.

Mr. Crowley shook his head, cupping his blood-soaked palm with his left hand. "You'll forgive me if I don't look so well. I'm a bit squeamish."

"Here. Come inside," Gemma said, ushering him into the house. "I'll get you some bandages to dress that."

After delivering him to the kitchen table decorated only with a vase of dead flowers, Gemma swiped a nearby towel and pushed it hard against Mr. Crowley's hand.

"Keep pressure on this," she said. "I'll go find some bandages in the bathroom."

Skirting into the bathroom, Gemma began rummaging through the closet filled with clean towels and toiletries.

"That happened so quickly," she called to him. "I didn't even see you cut your hand."

"Yes, quite suddenly," he called back to her from the kitchen. "I hope this isn't too much trouble."

Just as Gemma peeled back a small pile of towels, her hands found the first aid kit wedged in the rear of the closet. Snatching it from the shelf, she dashed back into the kitchen and dropped the kit on the table.

"No trouble at all," she assured him, opening the kit and fishing inside for some antiseptic ointment.

"You have a daughter?" Mr. Crowley asked.

Gemma's eyes snapped to him, her face scrunching. "How did you know?"

Mr. Crowley answered, gesturing to the kitchen counter where a framed photograph of Gemma's daughter, Piper, sat.

Gemma softened, lowering her guard. "Oh, yes. She's at a friend's house right now."

Finally, Gemma located the ointment and squeezed a little out, smearing it on Mr. Crowley's hand.

"This is going to sting a little," she warned him.

"It must be—unbearable—to have a child burdened with blindness," Mr. Crowley said, his eyes fixed on the photograph. "It must be—excruciating—to have something she'll never understand: eyesight."

Gemma reeled at the frankness of his comment. Of course, it had pained her every day to see her daughter treated differently than other children, but she scarcely needed the reminder.

"She's very special," Gemma said, forcing a polite smile as she dabbed more of the ointment onto Mr. Crowley's hand. "It's not as horrible as you may think."

"Of course, I never meant to offend," Mr. Crowley explained. "I just meant that it must be difficult for a mother to know her child will always be treated differently."

The brittle sound of Mr. Crowley's voice dimmed to a whisper in Gemma's ear drum. She wasn't even listening to him any longer; she couldn't bear the half-hearted sympathetic glances or the vaguely sincere pities. She merely wanted to dress his wound and get him on his way as soon as possible—anything to spare her the ugly reminder of her daughter's irreparable differences.

Just as she unspooled a roll of gauze from the first aid kit, Mr. Crowley rested his hand on her arm.

"You needn't trouble yourself with the dressings," he said to her.

She watched in silence as Mr. Crowley touched his injured hand, skin threading together like fine needlework and blood disappearing until his pruned hand was bone dry.

Gemma's mouth hung open in disbelief, watching the miraculous spectacle. "How did you—?"

She could hardly speak, her eyes glued to Mr. Crowley's healed right hand.

"What is it you want to know, my dear?" he asked her, smiling as if delighting in her wonderment. "There's certainly something I want to know."

Gemma shivered as he rose from his chair and approached her. "Yes?"

"If you could have anything in the world, what would it be?" he asked. "If the universe could grant your most unreasonable demand, what might you ask of it?"

Gemma's mind raced. Had she really just seen Mr. Crowley repair his hand with a mere touch? What was he? A creature from another world? Or perhaps something far worse?

Just then, her eyes snapped to the photograph of Piper on the kitchen counter—the dim milky white screens which hung behind both of her precious little eyes, the way her lips were parted as if in mid-laugh.

"I'd want my little girl to be able to see," Gemma said, quietly as if feeling foolish for voicing such an impossible thought.

"I can give her that gift," Mr. Crowley said. "I have that power."

Gemma shook her head in disbelief. It was too perverse to believe.

"I don't believe it," she said.

"You've seen what I can do," he said to her. "Shall I show you again?"

Mr. Crowley waved his hand over the vase of dead flowers. Stems began to straighten like the tightened strings of a virtuoso's violin.

Flowers sprouted upright, buds blooming until their blossoms were full and bright—desiccation in reverse.

"Still unsatisfied?" he asked her, plucking a flower from the vase and passing it to her as if for inspection.

She studied the flower in her hand. This was no trick of light, no paltry sleight of hand executed by an apprentice illusionist. This was sorcery.

"What do you want?" she asked, glaring at him.

"For you to come with me."

"Where?"

"I'll show you when we get there," he said, pulling gloves from his pocket and slipping them on. "We won't be but an hour. Your daughter will hardly miss you."

Gemma still wasn't convinced. She hesitated. "You can help her?"

"My dear, you've seen what I can do. You're still skeptical—?"

He stared at her, his eyes boring holes in her as if he were melting the steel walls she had built long ago to keep people like him out.

Gemma sensed herself soften, as if a warm hand had reached inside her and thawed what was once icebound, what was once numb.

"You promise we won't be long?" she asked him.

"I promise, my dear," he said, gesturing to the front door.

Gemma swiped her coat from the coat rack, her scarf and mittens, too, as she followed him out of the house. She thought of her precious daughter, wondered how it might be when she could finally see again. Her mind churned, imagining Mr. Crowley possessing her daughter with his charm, enchanting the blindness from her eyes and planting sight there as if it were as simple as scattering a mere seed to grow in a bed of fresh soil.

If Mr. Crowley were truly some rare winged species—some precious creature delivered by winds sent from a distant land as Gemma had thought—she wouldn't be surprised in the least. She couldn't be certain where he was taking her, but if it meant he could help Piper, she would follow him to the end of the earth—to a sacred place where the children's eyes were clear and cloudless, where daylight was everlasting, and where nighttime was a permanently cured disease nobody dared to speak of.

CHAPTER TEN

As they drove through the winding countryside, Gemma couldn't help but smell the curious scent of peppermint. The aroma seemed to fill the car. It wasn't that Gemma hated the smell. Quite the contrary. It had made her think of her grandfather, sitting on his lap when she was a little girl and listening to his stories of days now long since gone, left behind in the Old Country.

She sensed her entire body loosen, icy skin thawing and molten blood cooling as if her grandfather's gentle voice had coiled inside her like a velvet rope and whispered, "Don't be afraid. I'm still here, my sweet child."

Gemma couldn't help but wonder if her sudden softening was the work of Mr. Crowley's sorcery, if he had somehow crawled into her mind and was privy to the secret language she and her grandfather had once shared.

Her suspicious thoughts gave way to more cheerful memories on the front porch of her grandparents' house in New Hampshire, dragonflies buzzing past their heads in the summer heat. She thought of her grandfather in his favorite red checkered shirt, sliding his glasses further up his nose as he read to her from one of her favorite children's books.

The cheeriness was short lived, however, as it wasn't long before Gemma couldn't shake the overwhelming feeling that someone—something—was peering into her mind and watching her, gently stirring the bowl of her thoughts until her memories began to crust and blacken.

She strained to think of her grandfather—the color of his eyes, the shape of his nose, the way his hands had felt—but could conjure nothing. The thoughts had suddenly vanished, as if someone had yanked them from her head. Her mind, once a lavish rose bed, now reduced to an emptying gutter that swine wouldn't even consider drinking from.

Gemma, bewildered, stole a moment and glanced at Mr. Crowley, almost certain her thoughtlessness was the consequence of his dark magic. She glared at him with fury, but soon found her anger tempering until it was no larger than a grain of rice. She mindlessly began to covet the lines around his mouth and eyes until they resembled the scratches at the bottom of a teacup. She thought of a silver spoon, circling the bottom of a cup—going over the dark thin lines like the immeasurable loop of time, the nauseating ache of infinity.

Before she could attempt to make sense of the thought, Mr. Crowley's car pulled up to the front steps of a massive Tudor-styled manor.

"We've arrived, my dear," the old man said, dragging the keys from the ignition and lurching out of the vehicle.

Severed from her daze, Gemma's eyes peered out the car window and glanced up at the monstrous mansion staring down at her as if she were a mere insect.

"What is this place—?" she asked, her eyes drifting from the ornate parapets to the vaulted windows.

"This is my home, my dear," Mr. Crowley said, opening the passenger door and gesturing for Gemma to climb out. "My family home, I should say. The Crowley family has owned it for six generations."

Gemma shook her head, refusing to budge from her seat. "I didn't think we were... I don't think this is a good idea."

"My dear, we came all this way," Mr. Crowley said. "I thought you wanted to help your daughter."

"I do," she said, eyes avoiding him as he glared at her. "I just—don't want to go in there."

Just then, a dark shadow passed over Gemma's face as if a car's visor had been pulled down to block out the sunlight. A force she couldn't quite comprehend pulled her from the vehicle and brought her to her feet where she found herself standing in front of the entrance to the large house only a few moments later. Mr. Crowley was at her side in a matter of seconds, fishing in his pocket for the housekeys.

"You needn't be worried, my dear," Mr. Crowley assured her, forcing the key into the lock and twisting the door handle open. "This is going to be best for your daughter. I always keep my promises."

Although she protested in what remained of the theater of her imagination, Gemma drifted across the threshold and into the foyer as if she were being carried by a specter. She scanned the walls filled with relics of religious paraphernalia so primitive looking that she wondered whether or not they had been blessed by Christ himself. Wincing, she made awkward glances at the holy figures immortalized in stained glasswork dangling from the chandelier. The illustrated figures seemed to glare at her, storming the sanctity of her mind with their weaponry and pilfering the few precious things that remained.

"Where are we going?" she asked the old man as she was pulled along, as if trapped on an invisible conveyor belt. "You said you'd help my daughter."

"In good time, my dear," Mr. Crowley said, his voice commanding her to follow as he neared the cellar door. "There's something I have to show you first."

He dug into his pocket and pulled out a small gold-colored key. She watched him push the key inside the lock, the door creaking open and the cellar steps stretching out in front of her.

"I want you to see something very special," he said, holding out his hand for her to follow.

Her mind in decay as if moth-eaten, Gemma could scarcely speak. But she knew well enough not to go into the cellar. She shrank at the mere prospect of the old man's touch.

"I'm not going down there," she whimpered.

As soon as she was about to turn and make a sprint for the front door, her feet wouldn't move—it was as if they were glued to the place where she was standing. She strained, urging her body to move but some inexplicable force had its thumb pressed down on her, keeping her to itself as if she were a mere pet. Doors closed and locked inside her mind, the only one remaining open—the door to the cellar.

As she swallowed hard and struggled to pull from deep inside herself the will to move, Gemma sensed something warm pooling between her legs. She looked down, a dark stain blooming from where her legs met. Her cheeks flushed with heat, little beads of urine trickling down her thighs and circling her ankles.

She stammered, unsure what to say. Her mind had yet to be robbed of its politeness.

"I—I didn't think... I'm—so sorry I'm not..."

Mr. Crowley wrapped an arm around Gemma's shoulder as she trembled. "There, there, my dear."

The old man's voice warped and suddenly it sounded as if her grandfather was speaking to her—"You needn't worry, sweet girl. I'll clean the carpet later."

The thought left as suddenly as it arrived. To her, it felt as if an invisible hand had entered her mind and drawn a curtain to cover the pleasant memory of when her grandfather had comforted her after she had mistakenly spilled a cup of apple juice on the living room rug.

Mr. Crowley pulled Gemma from where she was standing. She did not resist anymore. Instead, she went with him willingly as if she were spellbound, her whole body under the influence of an accomplished magician. If there remained a tiny part of her mind to resist—a small insect to crawl out from beneath the curtain Mr. Crowley had drawn there—it certainly wouldn't be alive for long as he seemed to spirit more thought from her until her mind was completely withered.

"Come, my dear," he said, leading her down the cellar steps. "There's nothing to be afraid of."

With the very last bit of resistance squeezed from her thoughts, Gemma followed him without comment like a dutiful servant, or a zombified housemaid secured in invisible bondage. Any thought of retaliation passed through the sieve Mr. Crowley had fixed in her mind as if her thoughts were scalding hot bathwater.

As they approached the bottom of the cellar steps, Mr. Crowley guided Gemma's eyes to the dark corner of the room where the two walls met.

There, she saw it.

Every thought poured out of her like water from a mountain spring until her mind was an empty cavern, a deep crater where little planets had been collected in the world behind her eyes. She was suddenly nothing more than a broken tree branch set adrift in whitewater rapids, a mere pebble tossed from the top of a waterfall.

Her eyes went over and over the thing in the corner of the room, desperately trying to make sense of what she was seeing.

"Well—?" Mr. Crowley said, prodding her closer. "What do you think, my dear?"

Gemma opened her mouth to speak, but no sound came out. She swallowed, her eyes wide and unblinking like precious livestock about to be killed. Finally, a sound surfaced from the pit of her throat.

Her voice was pinched, brittle thin as if the very life were being choked from her. Still, she possessed the energy to utter two words before her mind went dark and oblivion finally claimed her.

"It's—beautiful," she said.

CHAPTER ELEVEN

When Malik returned home from work later that evening, he didn't notice how the French doors overlooking the patio had been pried open as if with a crowbar. He didn't notice the dark footprints running across the length of the white living room carpet, nor the broken glass discarded on the kitchen floor like a dowager's jewelry.

All of those things certainly could have told them something was wrong—that something had happened.

Even the sky had seemed to seethe, the heavens pulsing with a dark current as if it were a sign—something was wrong.

Malik somehow missed those signs.

It had already been done. There was nothing Malik could do.

He lumbered his way through the garage door and into the kitchen with his bag of groceries, dropping them on the counter.

"I'm back, babe," he shouted, his eyes scanning the dimly lit room. Of course, he thought it was peculiar. After all, Brett had always kept the place well-lit even during the daytime as per his psychiatrist's request on account of his seasonal depression. But he reasoned Brett was busy with work upstairs and somehow forgot.

"I bought some lamb for dinner," he said, beginning to unpack the bag and passing the perishables into the refrigerator. "I thought we could cook it with that sauce you like."

There was no response from the house. No sign of Brett.

He sensed his face scrunch, his eyebrows furrowing. It wasn't like Brett to not greet him when he returned home at a reasonable hour, even if he was still working.

Just as he took a step out of the kitchen and into the living room, he felt something crunch beneath his shoes. Lifting his foot, he peeled a shard of broken glass from the tread of his loafers.

"Brett?" he called out, looking around.

It was then he noticed a trail of shattered glass winding from the kitchen's tiled floor to the foot of the stairwell. As he slowly crept, following the trail of glass, he noticed picture frames on the walls battered and beaten. He passed broken vases on tables flipped upside down, flowers scattered across the hardwood floor and dripping wet like the bodies of drowned woodland sprites.

"Brett, please say something," he begged, turning the corner and creeping up the stairwell strewn with tattered bits of clothing. "Brett—?"

Nearing the top of the stairs, his eyes peered into the small office a few feet from the stairwell and it was there that he saw him—Brett curled on the floor like a child's doll discarded in a rainstorm, blood leeching across the carpet like a shadow.

Malik called out to him, rushing to his husband and tossing aside the broken furniture littering his path. He scooped Brett's body from the floor and wiped the blood-matted hair covering his face.

Both of Brett's eyes were dark and swollen shut, his lips fat and split apart like exploded grapes in sunlight, his forehead torn open and the crescent moon of his skull showing through the skin like wax paper. Malik cradled his husband in his arms, shaking him as if his mere embrace could patch the slit in Brett's forehead where blood leaked like tree syrup.

Malik shook him again, sensing Brett's body softening and going limp. Brett began to stir gently as if awakening. Shifting to try to find a modicum of comfort when there was none to be had, Brett flinched and sniveled like a fussing newborn.

"Babe," Malik exhaled, sponging the tears from his eyes. "What the fuck happened?"

Brett's swollen lips parted, blood webbing in the corners. He tried to speak, but there was no voice to donate the words. Malik glanced at Brett's throat and noticed dark bruising there, as if he had been strangled with a noose.

Malik leaned in close to Brett, his nostrils curling at the pungent odor of excrement. He wondered if in his panic during the attack Brett had soiled himself.

"Who did this to you?" Malik asked, dragging his husband closer to him.

He followed Brett's eyes to the office wall, and it was then he saw it. A single word smeared there with fresh excrement—FAGGOTS.

Malik phoned for an ambulance, and a paramedic team arrived along with the local police to survey the area. He watched helplessly as officers combed the scene, taking inventory of the remnants the assailants had left—the few battered pieces of his life that remained. Thankfully, Brett was one of those remaining pieces despite their best efforts.

Malik thought it was peculiar. He had always thought that if something ever happened to Brett, he would somehow feel it too—the same way that people say identical twins feel one another's agony. Malik was waiting for the moment when his ribcage would ache as if slashed or when his head would throb as if he had been beaten with the same crowbar they had used on his husband. But that moment didn't seem to come. That glorious moment of synergy—of a bond between two people in love—didn't seem to make itself known.

It scared him.

He wondered why he couldn't feel anything. He wondered why he couldn't seem to feel his husband's agony, or at the very least feel a sense of fury for those vile bastards who had tried in earnest to kill him.

Instead, Malik felt nothing.

He felt nothing during the ambulance ride to the local hospital when he watched paramedics strap an oxygen mask to his husband's face. He felt nothing as he watched behind glass doors as doctors and nurses flanked his husband's bedside after they had rolled him in.

He wondered if he would continue to feel nothing, if he had somehow been vacuumed out like a fuel tank.

What the fuck is wrong with me? he thought to himself, staring at his husband as he reclined in a hospital bed with blood-browned bandages covering his face and wires snaking through his arms as nearby machines recorded his vitals. *Why can't I feel something?*

He would have welcomed anything at this point—even the ugliest emotion to leech off of him like a tapeworm twisting in his intestines just so that he could feel something. He would have given anything to sense his cheeks heat with fury, to feel tears beading in the corners of his eyes. But it had been as though a deer tick had latched onto his body and drained him of any prospect of emotion—a fanged creature sucking the very energy from Malik until he was as vacant as dried-out honeycomb.

In his peripheral vision, he noticed a tall figure approaching him. He turned, watching Captain Chisholm making his way down the ICU corridor. The man's face was a mask of sorrow—lips pulling down, eyes lowered as if in deep respect.

For a moment, the two men stood in silence as they gazed into the small hospital room where Brett lay in bed, the poor thing's eyes closed as he drifted in and out of morphine sleep.

For the first time, Malik entertained a terrible thought—grabbing the Captain by the throat and smashing his head into the window until the glass cracked like an eggshell. He thought of dragging him to the ground, fists pummeling him until the Captain's head burst open like a melon strapped with explosives. Malik felt nothing as these thoughts arrived and then abandoned him as quickly as they came.

After all, that wouldn't undo the damage that had been done. That wouldn't mend Brett's wounds or dry the shit they had smeared in his mouth before they had left him there to die in utter humiliation. That wouldn't make Malik feel something no matter how desperately he wanted to.

He turned, studying Captain Chisholm for a moment, studying the kind of man he was. Or at least, the kind of man he thought he once was. The broad shoulders Malik had once revered seemed to lean inward, unconfident. Eyes that could command a room now appeared vacant, listless. Even if Captain Chisholm was filled with pity for Malik and his battered husband, Malik wouldn't dare accept his compassion. He'd sooner unplug the machines keeping Brett alive than feel a sense of fellowship with this Captain.

Malik glared at him, his eyes eviscerating him until he resembled the very thing Malik now thought of him—gutless.

"You still think we asked for this to happen?" Malik asked him.

Before the Captain could answer, Malik turned and left him standing there. He wasn't sure to where he was headed—the moon, the stars, another planet, any place but home—but he knew for certain that it would be somewhere he could feel something.

He wanted to hurt, and he wanted the feeling to last.

CHAPTER TWELVE

If Ghost had felt love for the little spirit curled on his shoulder like a sleeping kitten, any semblance of it was certainly gone now and had been gone for quite some time. Perhaps once he might have pampered the small creature, feeding it thoughts of misery and heartache it so desperately craved the same way a reptile handler feeds crickets and other dead insects to a red-bellied newt. Perhaps once the two might have existed in flawless harmony, the way certain parasites clean and nourish their hosts as they're fed in return.

Any possibility of companionship was gone now, however— the little creature taking more from him than he had ever received in return. Of course, Ghost had done much to temper the spirit's verve so that it didn't get in the way of his day-to-day life; however, any hint of camaraderie he had sensed with the little pest seemed to disintegrate whenever he considered calling Gemma and asking her to go for a walk as she had suggested when they first met.

"You know, she was only being polite," the wraith hissed, circling Ghost's face and plugging his nose and ears to search for any uneaten scraps of hopelessness it had left there. "Why on earth would such a lovely young woman want to get to know a miserable sack of shit like you?"

Ghost's eyes went over Gemma's number glaring at him from his cellphone screen. "She said she wanted to walk together sometime. She might be lonely, too."

"She isn't lonely. The stupid cunt felt sorry for you."

"Don't call her that," Ghost said, swatting the little spirit away. "She wanted to get to know me."

"She wanted to use you," the small creature said, coiling next to Ghost's shoulder.

"I have nothing to give," Ghost reminded the little spirit.

Of course, Ghost had wondered why Gemma had so quickly offered her phone number to him after a few moments. Perhaps she had admired the way he was with her daughter. He imagined some people were scared to approach, much less interact with a blind child.

The thing was, Ghost had felt a kinship with Piper the moment he saw her. They both were different—siblings of a similar sorrow. The only difference was Piper's affliction greeted you the moment you laid eyes upon her. For Ghost, you had to look a little harder to see the brokenness dwelling inside him. Regardless, it was still there and showed no signs of abandoning him yet.

"For fuck's sake, what would the two of you even talk about?" The wraith murmured in Ghost's ear, its voice wafting through him like black steam. "She doesn't care about you or your dead wife."

Ghost's eyes avoided the spirit as it drifted around his head, his eyes locked on his phone. "She's kind. She could be a good—distraction."

"Distraction? From what? Me?" The wraith laughed. "Trust me. You need me, you miserable bastard."

Ghost's finger hovered over the "call" button. "I'm going to do it."

"You'll regret it," the spirit warned him.

Without another moment of hesitation, Ghost pressed the button and held the phone to his ear. As it began to ring, the wraith leapt from shoulder to shoulder, hissing at him.

"It's not too late to hang up," the spirit said. "You're going to regret this."

But Ghost swatted it away once more as if the spirit were a nagging horse fly.

A man's voice greeted Ghost on the other end of the line.

"Hello?"

Ghost stammered, unsure. Who was this? Perhaps a lover? Or worse, a husband she hadn't mentioned. He thought of hanging up, but his voice answered before his fingers could.

"Yes. Hi," he whimpered.

"Who's this?" The man asked, voice hardening.

"I'm sorry. I'm calling for Gemma," Ghost said, wincing a little. "Uhh, I didn't get her last name. But we had met at the hospital a few weeks ago."

"Who's calling?" the voice asked.

"Ghost. My name's Ghost."

"Ghost?"

Ghost exhaled deeply, rolling his eyes. "Yeah. Like Halloween. Look, is Gemma there? Or maybe I can call another time?"

"She's not here," the voice replied. "Are you a close friend?"

"We only met once."

There was silence on the other end of the line.

"Has something happened? Is she OK?"

"Gemma left home last week and never came back," the man's voice explained. "I'm her brother, Tate."

"She's been missing?"

"For a week and a half now," Tate explained. "I don't suppose you know anything of where she could be."

Ghost sensed his breathing become shallower, his mind racing as he thought of Gemma's daughter alone and confused without her mother.

"No. I—I didn't know."

"She left her cellphone in the house before she left. I've been answering anytime it rings in case it's her," Tate explained. "I was hoping you might know something."

"I wish I did," Ghost said, flinching as the little spirit circled his head. "Is her daughter OK? Being taken care of?"

"I've been staying at the house and taking care of Piper," Tate said, drawing in a labored breath. "I'm afraid I can't really chat. You understand, I'm sure."

"Yes. Of course," Ghost said. "Thank you for letting me know."

Fingers flicking across his phone screen, Ghost ended the call.

He sat there for a moment in silence, the little wraith winging cheerfully about his head like a ladybug in the summertime. Everything around him seemed to slow as if his head were being held underwater. He thought of Gemma, wondering where she could have gone. He wondered if it had been too much for her—the unpleasantness of tending to a disabled child, the sympathies she'd forever receive from complete strangers. Although she had appeared joyful and carefree when he had met her, he reasoned that anyone was capable of putting on an act—playing the role of the dutiful mother while secretly resenting her child, perhaps even hating her.

It wasn't long before his thoughts turned to poor, sweet Piper—the small child with the broken arm and the seahorse balloon he had met so briefly. He thought of her alone, scared, bewildered—wondering why her mother had left her and perhaps coming to the horrible realization that her mother had abandoned her because she was a hideous, incurable monster. Ghost winced, tears beading in the corners of his eyes when he thought of Piper and how she must have suddenly realized that an earth-bound God—a mother—can abandon their creation after smearing them upon the face of the world.

Ghost felt sorry for Piper, but he recognized it was far better for the sweet child to learn this lesson now than to go through life being so trusting. After all, her world was darkness and that's often where the monsters felt most at home.

CHAPTER THIRTEEN

Ghost wasn't aware of the black Rolls Royce stalking him like a nocturnal predator. He didn't pay any mind to the vehicle as it cruised in front of his house in the morning when the neighborhood was still and quiet or when it idled in front of the supermarket while he shopped for groceries.

As Ghost limped onto the sidewalk, nearly dropping his cane, the car slowed to a crawl and pulled up alongside him, revealing a peculiar-looking old man outfitted with black driving goggles like an insect in the driver's seat.

"A thousand apologies," the old man said, lowering the passenger window and removing his goggles. "I didn't see you until it was too late."

"It's OK," Ghost said, waving the gentleman on and brushing off the dirt smeared on his knees. "No harm done."

The window lifted until Ghost could see his reflection in the dark glass. But the car didn't move. Just then, the window lowered once more, and the old gentleman leaned over in his seat as he called out to Ghost.

"You aren't waiting for a ride, are you?" he asked.

"Yeah. A cab's on the way."

The old man studied him for a moment, as if assessing how forward he could be. "I'm sure you may not believe it, given our recent history; however, I have been told I make an excellent chauffeur."

Of course, Ghost didn't believe him. Especially given the fact that the old man nearly ran him off the road.

"That's very kind of you to offer," Ghost said. "But the cab's already on its way."

"I won't charge you anything except polite conversation," the old man assured him, his hand patting the empty passenger seat.

Ghost's eyes scoured the old man for any semblance of dishonesty, a trick or deception—anything to tell him what he might be planning. His mind couldn't help but wander to grimly exaggerated notions— scenarios where the old man trapped and drained him until his body was bloodless. Or worse, a scenario where the old man would let Ghost live in agony and keep him for his perverted personal amusement. Despite the barrage of conspiracies Ghost had invented in such a short period of time, he couldn't help but be reminded of the lightness of his wallet. He wouldn't be able to tip the cab driver this time anyway and felt guilty for that sad realization.

"He's going to spear you on a spit roast and make jam of your intestines," the wraith whispered to Ghost as it circled his ear. "You're going to be his little bitch."

Ghost swatted the nuisance away until the spirit retreated, coiling inside his ear.

"You probably aren't headed where I'm going," Ghost said.

"My dear boy," the old man said, "I'm going exactly where you're going. Please. Don't be shy."

Against every instinct that screamed until hoarse inside his mind—every profanity that the tiny spirit curled around his throat had shouted at him—Ghost opened the passenger door and climbed inside the car.

"Very good, dear boy," the old man said, patting Ghost on the shoulder before easing his foot on the accelerator and peeling out of the hospital driveway.

After driving for a short while, Ghost noticed in his peripheral vision the old man eyeing him as if he were sizing him up and down the way a constrictor lovingly gazes at a meal.

"You aren't sick, are you?" the old man asked, as if suddenly concerned.

"Sick?"

"I suppose I should've asked you that before I offered to give you a ride," the old man realized. "I was just curious since you were at the hospital."

"No. I'm not sick," Ghost said, nervously fiddling with his cane between his legs. "Just a normal checkup."

Ghost watched the old man's eyes travel further down until they arrived at his cane.

"That's beautiful," he said. "I've always been envious of those who travel with companions."

The old man laughed, genuinely amused.

"I could do without certain company," Ghost said, glancing down at the little spirit as it circled his throat.

"I always say, 'if you can pay for company, what's the point in being alone?'"

Ghost sensed himself sinking further into the leather seat at the reminder of the empty house he was returning to—the loneliness he wished was nothing more than a distant memory now waiting for him.

"My name's Heart, if you were wondering," the old man said, eyeing Ghost as if waiting for a look of puzzlement. "Yes, like the thing that keeps us alive."

Ghost softened for a moment. Finally, someone with a name as questionable as his.

"I'm Ghost," he said. "Like Halloween."

"What do you do, Ghost?" Mr. Crowley asked, easing on the brakes as they neared a sharp turn in the road.

"Well, nothing since... Because of the..." his voice trailed off as he gestured to the cane.

"I imagine a man with a cane needs idle conversation like a Russian Empress needs an endless supply of Stroganoff," Mr. Crowley said, chuckling. "You see, I know what people need and what they don't need. That's the art of salesmanship—anticipating needs."

"You're a salesman?"

Mr. Crowley passed Ghost a small brochure from the car's center console.

"Carter Ridge Burial Plots," Ghost read as his eyes scoured the leaflet. "Begin your eternity today."

"Finest burial plots in New England," Mr. Crowley promised him. "Views—quite literally—to die for."

Ghost's eyes coveted the pictures of lush greenery printed on the brochure; the rolling emerald pastures flanked by headstones. He thought of his beloved Hailey and how the two of them should be together—surrounded by lush dreamscapes, eternity their only destination.

"You see, a good salesman knows exactly what their clients need," Mr. Crowley explained. "For instance, I know a young man such as yourself has no need to consider a burial plot at this stage in his life. Times are exciting. Life is vibrant and for the taking. What would you need to consider eternity for?"

Ghost was quiet. Of course, he had considered where he was going to spend eternity before. The little wraith around his throat had once told him that death is merely a dark room without doors and windows. As much as it hurt him to recognize this sad fact, there was the possibility that he might never see his beloved ever again.

"Why don't you try to stump me?" Mr. Crowley asked.

Ghost looked at him, bewildered. "Stump you?"

"Yes. Why don't you tell me what you most want in life? If you could have anything in the world, that is."

Of course, Ghost knew the answer intimately. It was to have Hailey in his arms once more—to comfort her and love her the way she deserved to be loved. But he wouldn't dare tell Mr. Crowley of his true desire. Something deep inside him told him not to. The little spirit whispered in his ear that Mr. Crowley wasn't to be trusted and that any mention of Hailey would insult the sanctity of her name.

Ghost eyed his cane. "I suppose—I'd like to be able to walk normally again."

Mr. Crowley rolled his eyes, unimpressed. "Oh, that's nonsense and you know it."

Ghost's eyes snapped to Mr. Crowley, shocked by the old man's brazenness.

"I know for a fact there's something else," Mr. Crowley said. "Something you're not telling me."

Ghost shifted in his seat, uncomfortable, as if Mr. Crowley's hands had reached inside him and were rearranging his viscera. No matter what, he wouldn't share what he wanted most of all—to be reunited with Hailey. It was too absurd of a notion to even consider, something Mr. Crowley would never understand no matter how accepting or receiving he was. He'd invent something—anything— to escape this loathsome conversation.

"I suppose I'd like to be free," Ghost said. "I have debt that's been following me around for a while and it would be nice to be free of that."

Mr. Crowley's eyes scanned him suspiciously up and down— distrustful, as if calibrating the truth of his claims.

"You're making my job quite easy, dear boy," Mr. Crowley explained. "What did I say about salesmanship? It's about anticipating needs."

"Yes—?"

"What would you say if I told you I could give you that freedom?" Mr. Crowley asked him. "What would you say if I told you I have the ability to make it so that you'll never worry about financial burdens ever again?"

Ghost merely shook his head, puzzled.

"Better yet, what would you say to five hundred thousand dollars?"

Ghost's eyes spiraled as soon as Mr. Crowley uttered the number. Suddenly, he realized he hadn't given his address to Mr. Crowley.

"I never told you where I lived," Ghost murmured, his mind seeming to curl as if being stroked by an invisible hand. "Where are we going?"

A monstrous house appeared beyond the tree line in the distance, rising into sight as if it were the ruins of an ancient civilization long since forgotten by mankind. Ghost's stomach dropped as the vehicle meandered toward the house and pulled up to the sweeping front steps.

"What is this place?" Ghost asked, his eyes glued to the giant home glaring down at him.

"The Crowley Estate. It's been in the family for five generations."

Ghost's mind raced to horrible, unimaginable thoughts. Perhaps the little spirit was correct—Mr. Crowley would split him open like a rotted melon and bathe in the surf of his blood. He knew for certain it would be the end for him if he stepped out of the car.

"I think you should take me home," Ghost said, straightening in his seat.

"Dear boy, I brought you all this way for a serious offer," Mr. Crowley explained, climbing out of the car and circling the vehicle. "The least you could do is join me inside and hear me out. That would be the polite thing to do."

But politeness was the last thing on Ghost's mind. He wouldn't budge in his seat, eyes avoiding Mr. Crowley as the old man tapped on the passenger window. Just as Ghost began to plot his escape, it felt as if an invisible leash had been wrapped around his neck and was pulling him out of the car. He was at the house's front door in a matter of seconds, Mr. Crowley flanking him.

"That's a good boy," Mr. Crowley said, patting him on the shoulder.

Ghost searched his mind for a thought of fear, a notion of dread—but all had suddenly been vacuumed from the pit of his consciousness. Doom seemed to abandon him and was gently replaced by a feeling of belonging, a gentle feeling that had already begun to heat his insides.

Mr. Crowley led Ghost inside the house and immediately lured him over to a credenza beside the entryway's ornate mirror embellished with glass illustrations of rosy-cheeked Boucher cherubs.

He opened the drawer and pulled out a checkbook and a fountain pen, already scrawling his signature on the dotted line.

"Half now," Mr. Crowley explained. "Half when you complete the assignment."

"What assignment—?"

Mr. Crowley's eyes cornered Ghost, his voice firming. "Something very delicate, dear boy. Something I wouldn't trust with just anyone."

"You hardly know me," Ghost reminded him, shrinking.

Mr. Crowley laughed, clearly amused by Ghost's incredulousness. "I know everyone I bring here intimately, dear boy. Why do you think I selected you?"

"Selected me?"

"I have been watching you," Mr. Crowley explained. "There's something about you—something I can't quite explain that makes you different. It makes you an exceptional candidate."

Once again, Ghost glanced at the tiny wraith as it circled his throat like a spurned honeybee—a thin wisp of smoke. He knew exactly what Mr. Crowley meant. Ghost had always been different, and he knew the horrible fact that others could tell, too.

"A candidate for what?" Ghost asked.

"For something I've conjured," Mr. Crowley explained. "Something I need to show you."

"Conjured?"

Ghost could scarcely believe the word. He looked at Mr. Crowley, dumbfounded.

"What are you?" he asked.

With a mere flick of his wrist, Mr. Crowley commanded the cane from Ghost's hand. The cane abandoned Ghost without comment, floating toward Mr. Crowley until it clattered at his feet. Ghost toppled over, sprawling on the floor like a dying insect. He watched as Mr. Crowley lifted the cane from the ground with merely his eyes and twirled the instrument in the air like a baton. Then, Mr. Crowley approached Ghost, towering over him as the cane floated above his head.

"I am magic," Mr. Crowley replied, lowering the cane from the ceiling until it touched the ground and stood beside Ghost's body.

Mr. Crowley offered his hand to Ghost to help lift him from the floor. Although Ghost was distrustful—eyes glaring at him—he swiped at the old man's hand and lurched off the ground until he was standing once more.

Then Mr. Crowley tore the note from the checkbook and passed it to Ghost.

"Half now, half when you finish," Mr. Crowley explained.

"Finish what?" Ghost asked, the cane trembling in his hand.

Mr. Crowley smiled, as if pleased Ghost had asked. "Come with me and I'll show you."

Without another word, Mr. Crowley turned and headed for the cellar door.

Ghost searched his mind for a reason to leave. But there was none. There were no words of warning from the little spirit tethered to his throat, there were no omens or admonitions detailing what butchery might possibly await him in the cellar. It was as if every pernicious thought had been ladled from his mind and disposed of. There was a small, quiet part of him that was curious—curious to see what monstrosities waited for him in the basement. He knew for a fact that nothing could harm him any more than he had already been.

Bracing himself, he began to inch down the cellar steps—ready and willing, like a virgin sacrifice to be eaten by the darkness.

CHAPTER FOURTEEN

A s they descended the cellar steps, darkness awaiting them down below, Ghost couldn't help but sense the air thicken with an electrical charge—a hissing current winging through the air like a tide of small nighttime insects. He wondered what gibbering, eyeless atrocities might await him—what Mr. Crowley was planning. He pondered unreasonable scenarios, wondering if Mr. Crowley were some type of advanced alien species and preparing to use him as his next host body. No matter the horrendousness of the thoughts that overwhelmed him, Ghost continued to inch down each step as if he were tethered to Mr. Crowley.

When they reached the final step, Mr. Crowley turned to Ghost and eyed him with an invitation.

"Well—?" he said, gesturing to the dimly lit space stretching in front of them.

Ghost squinted. In the darkness, he could barely make out the shapes of several people kneeling, their heads lowered respectfully as if in prayer. When he looked closer, he recognized one of the figures kneeling—it was Gemma. Her skin was as clear as wax paper, her hair soft-looking, like freshly spun cobweb.

Without hesitation, Ghost leaped across the room until he was at Gemma's side. He knelt beside her, gently stirring her.

"Gemma?" he said, shaking her limp body as if she were a mere rag doll.

"You know Ms. Carlisle?" Mr. Crowley asked, circling Ghost as he continued to rattle her body to no avail. "I had such high hopes for her. Of course, I have the utmost confidence in all of them when I first bring them here."

Ghost's eyes drifted to the others kneeling beside Gemma, their heads lowered and their lips moving with muted prayers. It was then that he recognized several of the other figures as people who had recently gone missing or had been missing from town for several months—Ms. Childers from the church thrift shop, Mr. Crenshaw from the bank. All were present and made up Mr. Crowley's grotesque collection.

"What have you done to them?" Ghost asked, the little wraith around his throat tightening its grip.

"It's not what I did to them, dear boy," Mr. Crowley said. "Look."

The old man gestured to a far corner of the room where two walls met. Ghost's eyes followed, widening when he finally saw it—a seething mass of energy floating in the corner. He rubbed his eyes in disbelief as he studied the formless shape as it swayed in place. The entity was a bright, glowing orb—an ornate latticework of veins and arteries sprouting from the center of the light like filament inside a bare lightbulb.

Ghost covered his mouth at the sight, rising from his knees and desperately trying to comprehend.

"What is it?" he asked.

Mr. Crowley was at his side in a matter of seconds.

"You believe in God, don't you?" the old man asked.

Ghost could hardly believe it. Was this thing—this churning mass of energy—was it really God? Of course, he had imagined the moment when he might come face to face with his creator, but he hardly expected that day might be today. He had planned every insult, every condemnation, every furious slur he could think of to chastise his creator for the life he had been given—for the pain he had been put through. But suddenly it was as if his mind had been wiped clean, a dark screen curtaining his every hateful thought.

"This—thing is—?" Ghost's voice trailed off, unsure.

"I told you I was magic," Mr. Crowley said, grinning.

Ghost's eyes returned to Gemma as she knelt before the glowing entity, her hands cupped together, and her eyes closed as if deep in prayer.

"What's happened to them?"

"They're worshipping Him," Mr. Crowley explained, milling through the rows of people kneeling as if they were tombstones. "I had brought each one of them here with the intent to complete a ritual. But their faith was too strong, and it's reduced them to mere zombies. Servants to their creator."

Ghost watched silently as a dark shadow of urine crept across the floor beneath one of the older women in the group. Mr. Crowley immediately swiped a mop and bucket from the nearby wall and began to scrub the floor.

"Of course, I do what I can to take care of them," he explained, "but I need to return them to the lives they once lived. To their families. To their loved ones. That's why I need you."

Ghost's heart whirled at the invitation.

"Me?"

"How do you feel?" the old man asked.

Ghost wasn't sure. He cleared the catch in his throat. "Fine, I guess. A little light-headed."

"But you don't feel the urge to submit yourself entirely to your creator?"

"And worship him?" Ghost asked. "For what?"

"That's precisely why you're the perfect candidate. You can help complete the ritual and help me return God to His rightful place in Heaven."

Ghost shook his head in disbelief. He stared at the glowing entity as it swirled in the corner of the room—scabbed with ancient constellations, crusted with distant galaxies now long since extinct.

"It can't be," he murmured, easing on his cane for support. He felt like he might fall over, but he would sooner die than submit to a creator—even if it wasn't truly God or at the very least, a kind of God—a lost deity.

"This thing—can't be God," Ghost said.

"You've seen it, haven't you?" Mr. Crowley asked, his eyes narrowing to mere slits as he gazed upon the bright glowing orb in the corner.

"If God is omnipotent, how come he didn't know you were going to conjure him?" Ghost asked.

Mr. Crowley's eyes lowered, as if filled with regret. "The ritual I performed to conjure God stripped Him of his powers. I'm afraid we haven't much time. The longer I keep Him here, the weaker He becomes."

"What do you need me for?"

"A sacred ritual to perform over the course of a month," Mr. Crowley explained. "You'll stay here at my home with me. We'll devote ourselves entirely to the ceremony."

Just then, he approached Ghost, his voice firming with a warning.

"Once we begin the ritual, we cannot stop. Do you understand?"

Ghost merely nodded. He pulled the crumpled check Mr. Crowley had given him from his pocket, staring at the numbers scrawled across the line.

"You'll pay the rest when we finish?" Ghost asked.

"You have my word," Mr. Crowley said, offering his hand.

Ghost hesitated. There was much to consider. Could Mr. Crowley really be trusted? Was this thing really the living embodiment of God on earth? Most importantly of all, would this ritual save Gemma?

His eyes drifted down to her as she knelt on the floor, unconscious of his every touch. He wanted her back from whatever astral plane she was currently inhabiting, wanted her to be with her daughter where she belonged.

Ghost's eyes returned to Mr. Crowley. He offered him his hand.

"You have my word, too," Ghost said as their hands touched.

Mr. Crowley's hand felt coarse and bristly, as if Ghost were shaking hands with a tarantula.

After Mr. Crowley had gone back up the cellar steps, Ghost turned and gazed upon the swirling mass floating in the basement's corner like the headlight of a ghostly locomotive. He still wasn't sure what the thing was—if it truly was some kind of lesser God, or inferior deity.

Regardless, he was pleased to know that when he left the cellar, he'd be leaving Gemma with a little bit of light.

PART THREE

IF WE WERE MADE OF HONEY

"Towards thee I roll, thou all-destroying but
unconquering whale; to the last I grapple with thee;
from hell's heart I stab at thee; for hate's sake I spit
my last breath at thee."

—Herman Melville, *Moby Dick*

CHAPTER FIFTEEN

After five days in the Intensive Care Unit, Brett was deemed fit enough to be relocated to another wing of the hospital where he could undergo therapy and receive visitors. Malik was always there at his husband's bedside until the night shift attendants arrived and ushered him on his way for the evening.

Brett had told the police everything he could remember of the assault—though his memory was filled with holes as if his mind were still reeling from the crowbar that had gone to work on his head. He had explained to authorities that he didn't see any of the assailants' faces as they were wearing black ski masks, that they had crept into the house and had surprised him as he was working in the office. He had told the police that there were three men—all of them dressed in black tactical gear as if prepared for combat.

Although the authorities guaranteed Brett and Malik that they would do all they could to locate the perpetrators responsible for Brett's attack, Malik couldn't help but sense their assurances were as and had distanced himself from the department, he knew full well that the Henley's Edge police force had more pressing engagements than a couple of frightened, battered homos. The residents continually reported missing remained at the top of the list.

"It's not fair," Malik said while he gazed out the rain-blurred window in Brett's private room. "They won't help us."

"They said they would do everything they could to catch them," Brett reminded him, wincing in pain as he stirred.

"Do you need something?" Malik asked, noticing his husband's private agony. "Should I call for the nurse?"

"No, no," Brett said, shooing him away. "It's just—hard to get comfortable."

Malik could understand. Every time he looked at Brett, he flinched in distress. Not because of sadness or even because of acrimony at the horrible reminder of his husband's suffering. It was merely because Brett's once glorious face—the face that had lit up Malik's entire world—was now hidden by bandages and dressings to cover the swelling. Whenever Brett would remove the dressings, Malik would wince a little at the grotesque reminder. Poor Brett's exposed face resembled a dog that had pushed its snout into a hornet's nest. Or, even worse, it resembled an action figure that had been melted and reshaped by a cigarette lighter.

"They're not doing anything to help us," Malik said, folding his arms as he paced the small room. "They act as if you deserved what happened to you."

Malik's eyes drifted to Brett, noticing him softening quietly.

"Don't you care?" he asked him.

"Of course, I do," Brett said, flinching while he strained to reach for a cup of water on the nightstand.

Malik beat him to it, passing the cup to Brett's mouth and holding it for him as he took a drink.

"There's something I've been thinking about," Malik said, setting the cup of water down on the tray in front of Brett and circling the bed. "Something I've been considering every night I go home on my own. Something you may not understand."

Brett looked at Malik blankly, as if expecting the worst. "Yes?"

A nurse dashed by the open doorway, startling Malik. He leapt across the room and closed the door. Then, when he was certain they wouldn't be disturbed, he returned to his husband's bedside.

"I've been thinking of leaving the department for good," he said quietly.

"Leaving? For good?"

"Yes," Malik said. "I just—don't think I can bear it any longer. They want me to be something I'm clearly not."

Brett winced in discomfort, straightening himself. "But you are. You always have been."

Malik lowered his head. There was something else. Something he could hardly admit to himself in the quiet of an empty house, let alone to his beloved husband. Of course, he had entertained the thought for quite some time—ever since Brett was first injured—however, finding the right words to pair with his inexplicable thoughts was an art form in and of itself.

"There's something else I've been thinking about," he said, eyes avoiding Brett at all costs. "Something I can't believe I'm considering. Something that—scares me."

Brett breathed a little more heavily, unsure. "What is it?"

Malik let the room fill with silence for a moment, uncertainty pluming all around him before he spoke again.

"I've been thinking of going after them myself," he said. "Tracking each of them down. Finding out where they live. Then, in the middle of the night, going into their homes and taking a baseball bat to their heads while they sleep."

Color drained from Brett's face. He spoke slowly, carefully considering every word as if Malik were a powder keg that could go off at any moment. "Have you told anyone else what you're thinking of doing?"

Malik merely shook his head. "You're the first person I've told. I've been thinking of hammering nails into the end of the baseball bat just so that it hurts them more."

"And when you think these things—how do you feel?" Brett asked.

Malik was surprised at the question. He hadn't truly considered how it had made him feel. Of course, the violent thoughts frightened him and seemed to drip in the corners of his brain like black tar. But he wanted vengeance more than anything—he wanted them to suffer just as they had made him and Brett hurt.

"It scares me sometimes," Malik said, cupping his hands together as if in prayer. "Makes me wonder if I'm capable of doing something so horrible. Part of me wants to know what it would feel like."

"But that's not you," Brett told him. "That's not the man I married."

Malik lowered his head again, eyes trained on the floor. "Maybe it is."

His eyes shifted to Brett who seemed to be rehearsing something unsaid, something that lingered between his lips purple with bruising.

"There's something I've been thinking about, too," Brett gently said. "Something I've been wanting to tell you for the past week."

Malik braced himself, sitting on the corner of the bed.

"Yes—?"

"I'm not going to break apart like fine China if you have to go back to work," Brett told him. "In fact, I think you should. I think it would be good for you."

"Good for me? To leave you and pretend this never happened?"

"You wouldn't be leaving me," Brett reminded him. "You have to let these doctors take care of me."

Malik shook his head in disbelief. "I can't believe you're saying this. Don't you want to find the people who did this to you?"

"I want to forget it ever happened," Brett said. "I don't want to be reminded of it anymore. I want you to forget about it, too."

"Forget?"

Malik could hardly believe what Brett was saying.

"I think you should go back to work," Brett said. "I think that would be best for both of us."

Malik sensed a pain in the center of his chest, a dull ache that began to spread. "You don't want me here every day?"

"Of course, I want you here with me," Brett said, grabbing his hand and rubbing it. "But I know you're not happy here. It's changing you. I think it would be best if you went back to work and did what you do best."

"What I thought I did best," Malik corrected him.

"Still do."

"You're prepared to just let everything go?" Malik asked in disbelief.

"I'm not letting anything go," Brett reminded him. "I'm letting you go to work."

"All they care about are those missing people—the old lady from the thrift store."

"You used to care about them," Brett said, pushing Malik's hand away until it was folded in his lap. "I think you still do."

Malik said nothing.

"You feel like a monster when you think these horrible thoughts, don't you?" Brett asked.

Malik merely nodded.

"I think going back to work and helping people would make you feel human again," Brett said.

Malik hated to admit it, but perhaps Brett was right. Even in his husband's morphine fever, Brett made better sense than Malik's internal dialogue for the past week and a half. He came to the realization that he cared for those who had gone missing, he felt compassion and sympathy for the loved ones they had left behind. At least Brett was still alive and present. He quietly thanked God for little mercies such as that.

Still, there was a quiet, undisturbed part of him—moored somewhere deep in the darkest recesses of his soul—that confessed in despair that he had no longer wished to feel human. To him, there was no longer anything appealing about the prospect of his humanity. That secret part of him—armored with spikes like a venomous insect—only wanted to feel something. That part of him wanted to find the men responsible for Brett's torment and grease his hands with their blood. Malik was scared to admit to himself what he truly wanted from them and even in his quietest moment of heartache he couldn't bear to utter the word—revenge.

CHAPTER SIXTEEN

After Ghost went home to collect some of his belongings, Mr. Crowley returned him to the estate and guided him to the east wing of the manor where he would be staying. Though Ghost was convinced the Crowley family had a considerable amount of wealth given their ostentatious decorations, he reasoned that funds went to areas other than housekeeping. The entire guest bedroom was blanketed in dust, spare furniture piled in the corner of the room—an atrociousness of excess. Though Ghost wasn't one to complain about accommodations, he felt sick as he swatted away cobwebs from the bed's headboard.

"It would mean a great deal to me if you would join me for dinner tonight," Mr. Crowley said as he milled at the guest bedroom doorway. "Eight o'clock?"

Ghost nodded.

Mr. Crowley's mouth creased with a small smile, as if hopeful—as if content to finally entertain company.

When he left, Ghost couldn't help but wonder if he had made a mistake—if this entire exercise was a ruse or worse, something to trap him and render him as useless and as zombified as the people in the cellar. Could he trust Mr. Crowley? Ghost wasn't convinced.

After supper, Mr. Crowley invited Ghost to retire with him in the library with a glass of brandy. Though Ghost explained he was still nursing a headache, Mr. Crowley insisted and before Ghost knew it, he was seated in front of a roaring fire while Liberace records played softly in the background.

"You enjoy Liberace?" Mr. Crowley asked, pouring Ghost a small glass of brandy.

Ghost shrugged. "I suppose."

"I always wish I could have played like him. But I never had the encouragement of a devoted parent—a benefactor, anything—to dedicate myself entirely to a craft," he explained as he served Ghost. "I would've given anything to play for audiences in Vienna like Mozart or entertain crowds in Paris like Chopin."

Suddenly, his eyes narrowed at Ghost. "Do you know what the difference between me and those gentlemen is?"

Ghost thought for a moment, surprised by the question.

"The difference is in the upbringing," Mr. Crowley explained. "Specifically, parents. Parents are godlike to children, aren't they? Parents are creators."

"Yes, I suppose they are," Ghost said, somewhat uncertain.

"A great composer—an extraordinary creator of art, literature, music—needs to be nurtured by another exceptional creator. Do you understand?"

Ghost nodded, although he couldn't be certain what Mr. Crowley was trying to say.

"I never had that," Mr. Crowley said, his eyes lowering. "Instead, I had a mother who named me 'Heart' because hers was broken."

Ghost leaned forward in his seat, struggling to understand.

"The man she had intended to marry left her four months before I was born," Mr. Crowley explained. "I was a painful reminder. I was a dark stain she had smeared on the world. Sent away to private school until I was eighteen because I was too much for her to bear. Too hideous of a reminder."

"Reminder of what?" Ghost asked, somewhat surprised by his curiosity.

"A reminder of what she had created," Mr. Crowley explained, glowering at him. "Just because you create something doesn't mean you have to take care of it."

Ghost couldn't relate. After all, his beloved creation had been taken away from him, ripped from the warmth of his wife's dead womb when the doctors had sprawled her lifeless body out on the operating table. The life he had once created had been torn away from him, but he reasoned he would never have abandoned something he had formed, something he and his wife had conjured with tenderness together.

"That thing I summoned in the cellar is proof of it," Mr. Crowley continued. "It doesn't care about the world it has created, the people in it who are suffering. Like all living things, it merely wants to survive."

Ghost hesitated to ask, but the question begged an answer.

"If that's the way you feel, then why are you so determined to help Him?" he asked.

Mr. Crowley straightened in his chair, both surprised and impressed with Ghost's brashness.

"Because it's my fault He's been sent here," the old man explained. "I invited Him here."

Mr. Crowley looked mournful, as if burying the regret deep inside himself where no mourners—no little spirits with appetites for suffering—could find it.

"I suppose I don't have the heart to abandon something after I've started it," he explained, downing the rest of his glass. "Not even God deserves that."

Drawing in a labored breath, Mr. Crowley rose from his seat and moved over to the record player to shut it off.

"I do hope you'll get some rest this evening," he said to Ghost. "We begin work tomorrow night."

Without the fanfare Ghost had come to expect from the old man, Mr. Crowley slipped out through the door and disappeared down the corridor until he was gone from view.

Ghost sat alone in the library, the unfinished glass of brandy swirling in his hand. His eyes drifted up the library wall and arrived at a giant wooden crucifix staring down at him from its sacred place above the mantle. Although his eyelids felt heavy, it wasn't long before the little spirit around his throat began to curl inside his ear and whisper to him that he would not be sleeping tonight.

CHAPTER SEVENTEEN

For many nights, the prospect of sleep remained an elusive creature to poor Malik—something whispered about, something only heard of but never seen, like an extinct species, a casualty of time. He wondered if he ever might find rest again, the very thought of lowering his guard in the privacy of an empty house seemed too foolhardy to even consider. If and when he did drift off to sleep for a few moments at a time, his dreams were often alarming and did very little to comfort his troubled mind.

He dreamt of his beloved Brett—somehow suddenly toothless and stuffed with straw like a farmhand's precious scarecrow. He'd wake up in a panic, drenched in cold sweat, and would reach for Brett's side of the bed only to be met with a small pile of pillows he had arranged there to make sleeping alone a little more bearable.

He realized it had been many years since he'd slept alone. He had grown accustomed to the sounds of Brett as he slept—the soft gurgling in the pit of his throat, the quiet whimpers as he rolled over onto his side or forced away a bad dream. Malik conceded he didn't quite know who he was without Brett—didn't quite understand where he stood in the cosmos or even if he was able to tolerate his own company. After all, he and Brett had met early on in college so many years ago and it had been a fairly speedy courtship until, before they knew it, they shared the same bed and housekeys.

He knew quite instantly that Brett was the one he was meant to be with, despite the thought of his devout Muslim grandparents' disapproval. Even though he willed himself to think that they might look favorably upon his decision to love freely, there was a part of him that always knew they would have detested who he was and how he was engaging in what they might have deemed "unconcealed perversion." After all, to add insult to injury—Malik was willingly going to bed with someone outside the Muslim faith.

Still, there was a secret part of him that couldn't help but wonder—couldn't help but wonder whether or not they would still love him as devoutly as they did when he was a child, when his sexual character was as indistinct as a lightning bug during a windstorm.

On the morning of the day when Malik was supposed to go to the hospital and retrieve Brett and finally bring him home, there was a knock at his front door. Always on guard, Malik eyed the baseball bat he had leaned against the coat closet door as he approached the entryway. Peering out the window, he was met with a brightly colored neon headband securing a nest of prematurely greying hair.

Malik opened the door and found Mr. Reiling, dressed in his usual neon tracksuit, filling the frame as he jogged in place.

"Good morning," Malik said, unsure how to properly greet the old man.

After all, he had, of course, seen him jogging in the neighborhood, but had never been formally introduced.

"Mr.—Malik?" the old man said, referring to a small notecard in his hand.

"Yeah, that's me."

"I was told what happened the other week," Mr. Reiling said, pocketing the notecard and slowing his pace until he was perfectly still. "We were so sorry to hear."

Malik couldn't help but notice how Mr. Reiling occasionally seemed to glance over his shoulder—as if he were being watched by some distant observer, as if he were fearful he might be caught talking to Malik, or worse, fearful he might be followed.

"Thank you. That's very kind of you," Malik said.

"Are you going out?" the old man asked, inching closer toward the threshold as if determined to enter the house with or without invitation.

He seemed to recognize his disrespect and shrank as Malik eyed him.

"Apologies," he said, lowering his head. "I was just—I was wondering if you had a moment. There's something I think you should know."

The words were like an icepick stirring Malik's brain. *Something I think you should know*, he repeated silently to himself. What possibly could it be? Malik, of course, expected the worst.

"I have a few minutes, I guess," Malik said, opening the door further.

"May I come in?"

"Please."

Mr. Reiling scurried into the house, dragging the door shut after him and peering out the window as if to make certain whoever or whatever was watching could no longer see him.

"Is everything OK?" Malik asked, cautious not to approach the old man any further.

"I'm afraid not," Mr. Reiling said, curtaining the window with drapes. "May we sit down?"

Malik led him into the living room where they sat.

"I'd offer you something to eat or drink, but I haven't gone to the store in a while now," he explained.

"That's quite alright," the old man said, his eyes darting around the room like a trapped animal. "I can't—won't be staying long."

"You said there's something you think I should know?"

Mr. Reiling swallowed hard, wetting his lips before he spoke. "I assume the neighbors have been less than cooperative with the police regarding your—situation?"

"They—don't seem to know much. Didn't see anything the night it happened."

"They're lying," Mr. Reiling said, biting his nails. "You know that, don't you?"

Of course, Malik had his suspicions. But he could hardly believe they were true, at least according to Mr. Reiling.

He leaned forward in his chair. "You know something?"

"They'd have my guts on a platter if they knew I was here with you right now," Mr. Reiling said, glancing over his shoulder and chewing on his thumb. "It was the lot of them. They ordered it to be done."

Malik sensed his breathing growing shallower. "Ordered what?"

"They wanted to scare you. Force you out of the neighborhood the only way they knew how," Mr. Reiling explained. "The intention was never to hurt anyone. They just—wanted to scare him. But the men they hired—"

"Hired?"

"Yes, a couple of men from Hartford County," Mr. Reiling said. "But they got carried away with it. They never meant for anyone to get hurt."

"You were a part of it?" Malik asked him, his face heating red.

"Never. I'd never—"

"Were you fucking part of it?" Malik asked, leaping out of his seat and barreling down on the old man. "Don't fucking lie to me, you old sack of shit."

Mr. Reiling squirmed, pinned against the couch as Malik pressed against him.

"I swear I wasn't," he said, wincing. "But I know the men responsible. I know who they are."

"Names," Malik said, pushing the old man further into the cushions. "I want fucking names."

Mr. Reiling struggled, slipping a quivering hand into his sweatshirt pocket. He pulled out a crumpled note and passed the paper to Malik.

After Malik backed down from the old man and uncrumpled the note, he found a name scrawled on the small scrap of paper: Saint Fleece. Beneath the name was the address of a bar on Railroad Street in the town of New Milford, Connecticut—a twenty-minute drive from Henley's Edge.

"Saint Fleece? Who is he? The patron saint of seamstresses?"

"He's a tall man with a dark goatee," Mr. Reiling explained. "He

145

and his men are regulars at that bar. You can ask for him. They'll know who he is."

Malik's eyes went over the name on the note again and again—Saint Fleece. What kind of name was that? Most certainly, the kind of name of a man he'd like to kill.

Without another moment of hesitation, Mr. Reiling sprang up from the couch and crept toward the front door.

"I'm afraid I can't stay," he said. "If they ask, I wasn't here. I never gave you that address. Do you understand?"

"You're in no position to be giving me demands, you spineless fuck," Malik said, crumpling the note.

"Please," the old man begged. "Do you know what they'd do to me and my wife if they knew I came here to talk to you?"

Malik recoiled for a moment, considering Mr. Reiling and the frailty of his much older wife. Of course, he'd never wish them the same agony and cruelty he and Brett had faced—even if they were guilty.

"I was never here," the old man said, flying out the door and down the front pathway.

After Malik watched the old man disappear from view, his eyes returned to the small note scrawled with the name and the address. He went over the name again and again—Saint Fleece—until the curve of every letter was blistered into his memory. Gritting his teeth, he squeezed the paper in his fist until the name was nothing more than a dark ink stain in his palm, until the name belonged to him and him alone.

CHAPTER EIGHTEEN

Ghost awoke and found himself alone in the house. He peered out one of the windows overlooking the driveway and found Mr. Crowley's car missing. Although Mr. Crowley had cautioned him about going into the cellar unaccompanied, he could hardly keep himself from thinking the thought. After all, sweet Gemma was down there—trapped. More precisely, genuflecting, silently revering that strange orb hanging in the cellar's corner.

Creeping down the cellar steps, Ghost came upon the rows of worshippers kneeling and admiring the glowing thing that swayed in midair where the two walls met. He weaved through their bodies, avoiding areas slimed with fresh excrement or damp with urine, until he came upon Gemma. Although he had hoped she might, she didn't seem to notice him as he milled beside her—her head fixed between her knees, as if she were in the presence of divine royalty. Perhaps she was. Although Ghost had seen the thing in the cellar, he still wasn't convinced Mr. Crowley had conjured the living embodiment of God

"Gemma," he whispered, gently nudging her.

She did not respond. Her head remained buried between her knees as her lips moved in silent prayer.

"Gemma," he repeated, tapping her shoulder. "It's me. Ghost."

But she wouldn't budge. Wouldn't even look at him.

When Ghost was quite certain Gemma wouldn't break from her zombified trance, his eyes drifted to the glowing orb of light swaying beside the cellar wall. Was this thing really God? He couldn't help but allow his mind to wander. What if it was? What if he were standing in the presence of an immortal deity? He sensed his stomach curling with hatred at the mere thought—the mere notion of the object of his disdain existing within arm's reach. Even worse, the mere thought that this thing—whatever it was—had the intention of taking another loved one away from him.

He approached the circle of light, his hands curling into fists.

"You'll excuse me if I don't bow," he said. "I'm not convinced you deserve such a warm reception."

The light did nothing. It hovered in place without comment.

Ghost sensed the little spirit curling around his throat, tightening as if with a warning—the same way all woodland creatures seem to know when a violent storm is approaching. He paid the spirit no mind, gently approaching the light in the cellar's corner.

He reached into his pocket and pulled out his wallet. From his wallet he tore out a small grainy picture of Hailey he had kept since she had first passed. He held the picture up to the light.

"This is Hailey," he said, voice shaking. "You killed her. You let her die."

Ghost winced, wiping away tears as they webbed in the corners of his eyes.

"You're a murderer," he said. "That's what you are. "You don't deserve the right to create. You don't get to create something and then walk away from it. That makes you a monster."

Ghost noticed how the light seemed to dim as he spoke, the halo of brightness shortening along the wall and beginning to fold inward like rose petals.

"I'd fucking annihilate you if I could," Ghost said.

"Is that so—?"

Ghost turned and found Mr. Crowley standing at the foot of the cellar steps, watching him.

"Mr. Everling, I'd caution you to use your words very carefully when addressing your creator," Mr. Crowley said, weaving through the bodies of worshippers. "After all, the tables will turn when we finish our ritual and God's returned to his heavenly throne. I'd hate for Him to bear a grudge because you were so careless with your language."

Ghost chuckled at the mere notion. "You think I care? I'd welcome a challenge from Him. He can destroy me for all I care— hammer me like a fresh chicken, grind me up until I'm nothing but powder. He'd be giving me exactly what I want."

"I think you'll come to feel differently when your head's on the slab, dear boy," Mr. Crowley said.

An older worshipper—Gus Crenshaw—suddenly raised himself from kneeling and released a deep, guttural groan like the sound of an animal in the throes of death. Ghost shuddered at the sound, Mr. Crenshaw's deafening groan reaching up inside him and rattling him as if he were a tin can. He watched in silence as Mr. Crowley approached the potbellied man with arms raised in the air like a penitent sinner seeking forgiveness at the feet of a holy man.

"Mr. Crenshaw?" Mr. Crowley said, nudging him.

Mr. Crenshaw's eyes snapped open suddenly, his head swiveling in every direction. He seemed to soften when he noticed Mr. Crowley loitering beside him, his breathing slowing to a mere murmur.

"Honey," Mr. Crenshaw whispered. "Honey, honey."

Ghost leaned in closer, unsure if he had heard the old man correctly.

"He's saying 'honey'?"

"I need honey," Mr. Crenshaw murmured, dragging Mr. Crowley's ear against his chapped lips. "I need all the honey you can find."

"Why's he saying that?" Ghost asked.

Mr. Crenshaw pulled Mr. Crowley closer again. "I need to transform myself until my body is a gift for Him. I need to mellify."

Mr. Crowley tugged on the old man's sleeve. "Mr. Crenshaw, I—"

"Please," the old man said. "I beg of you."

As quickly as he sprang from his trance, Mr. Crenshaw returned to kneeling and continued his silent prayers as if he were compelled to obey a command issued by some unseen, all-knowing force.

"What was he saying?" Ghost asked.

Mr. Crowley drew in a labored breath. "He wants to self-mellify."

"Mellify?"

"It's an ancient custom of self-sacrifice practiced in some Middle Eastern countries where the body is soaked entirely in honey."

Ghost could hardly believe it. "He wants to—?"

"Yes. As an offering," Mr. Crowley explained. "That's why we need to make haste with the ritual. To prevent these poor people from hurting themselves for the sake of their creator."

"What should we do?"

"I'll send you to the store to fetch all the honey you can find," Mr. Crowley said.

"But we'd be letting him die."

"It's just to placate him," Mr. Crowley explained. "We'll finish the ritual before he can even begin the process."

But Ghost wasn't convinced.

"You're sure it won't harm him?"

"Hurry up, dear boy," Mr. Crowley said, hastening up the cellar steps, ignoring his question. "There's so much work to be done before we begin the first ritual tonight."

Stealing a moment to regard his beloved Gemma, Ghost inched toward her and brushed some of the hair from her face. She said nothing, her eyes vacant and milky white like her daughter's.

"Promise me you'll never ask to bury yourself in honey for a God that doesn't care," he said to her.

Just as he was about to peck her forehead with a kiss, Mr. Crowley called to him from further up the stairwell. Ghost dragged himself after the old man like an obedient dog, like a poor creature that knew full well his owner would turn on him if he refused to obey.

CHAPTER NINETEEN

Much to the dismay of the voices inside his head imploring him to reconsider his plan, Malik swiped a large knife from the kitchen counter and climbed into his car to make the twenty-minute trek to the bar in New Milford. As he drove, he imagined the different scenarios of how things might transpire between the two of them, the things he would say to Saint Fleece before attacking him and making him pay for what he had done to his beloved Brett. He imagined pinning the man to the ground and watching him squirm like a rodent—a creature so pathetic and so helpless that Malik could barely feel pity.

Eyeing the knife in the passenger seat as he drove, Malik wondered if he actually possessed the skill to make good use of it. Of course, it was one thing to think about performing horrible acts on deserving scum like Saint Fleece, but it was another thing to actually carry through with it. He wondered if his resolve might weaken, if he might feel a semblance of pity for the man when the time came.

Although he had played out the moment countless times in the privacy of his thoughts before sleep, he couldn't help but wonder if he would actually go through with it. There was a voice—insidiously small and yet impossibly perceptible—begging him to turn the car around and return to the hospital to be with Brett. At every red light, at every moment when Malik's foot eased on the brake, the voice spoke to him and urged him to forget the plan. If you could even call it a plan.

Malik had no words prepared. He had no actions rehearsed, no expertise when it came to wielding a knife. Of course, the department required him to carry a firearm on his person at all times. But with crime being what it was in Henley's Edge—there was never an opportunity to use it. Violence was a language he seldom spoke.

After all, he hadn't been in a fight since grade school, when Spencer Gracey had called him an "Allah-loving faggot" during recess. Malik wasn't even certain what he hoped to gain from meeting the man responsible for his husband's suffering. Yes, perhaps it was to hurt him as he had hurt them. But, more importantly, Malik realized that he wanted to scare him—wanted to turn his hair white and curdle his blood. He wanted him to suffer, too.

After a twenty-minute drive, Malik pulled his car into the bar's parking lot on Railroad Street and parked further down the lot near the abandoned train tracks drowning in weeds. Malik didn't think it was strange for the lot to be so empty, especially in the early afternoon when most people were working. His eyes drifted to the neon sign hanging beside the small building's entrance—STATELINE TAPROOM & BAR glowing in bright green lettering. Crowding near the entrance was a small group of men—all dressed in baggy clothing, some with tattoos, others without. Malik searched each and every one of them for a sign—a signal that they were the abomination known as Saint Fleece.

Mr. Reiling's words hummed in his head: *"A tall man with a dark goatee."*

Scanning each of the men near the building's entrance, he was met with disappointment. Saint Fleece was certainly not among them.

It was then he noticed a red Subaru with dark, tinted windows parked beside the building's dumpster. He had finally found it—the vehicle that had been cruising his neighborhood on the same night of the first attack. Snatching the knife from the passenger seat and pocketing it, he climbed out of his car and slowly made his way across the lot toward the Subaru. The men milling near the bar entrance noticed him but seemed to think nothing of him as he circled the parked car, peering through each of the windows.

"Hey," Malik called out to the group of men huddled beneath the building's neon sign. "You know who owns this car?"

"Hey, Saint," one of the men called into the bar. "Someone out here's asking about your car."

It was then Malik knew he had found him. He didn't hesitate a moment. Swiping the knife from his coat pocket, he knelt and stabbed at the rear tire. Again and again until he heard a soft whistling sound. Then, he scurried to the front tire and stabbed that tire until he was content. He could hear the men near the building's entrance calling out to him, urging him to stop—but he paid them no mind. Not until he noticed a tall gentleman with a dark beard emerge from the building dressed in dark clothing, his eyes secreted behind sunglasses.

"This crazy fuck just slashed your tires, man," one of the men said to him as he passed them.

This was the moment Malik had been waiting for. He had invented scenarios of this moment in his mind for so long, but there was something quite different when it was actually happening as the tall man with the goatee approached him. The world around him seemed to slow, all noise dimming to a soft hum like a distant beehive.

"I think we have a problem here," the man said to Malik as he came upon the car, noticing the deflating tires.

Malik nodded. He sensed the knife tremble in his hands, and he knew the tall man recognized the hesitation etched in his face.

"Are you—Saint Fleece?"

The man flaunted a graveyard of decaying teeth at him. "I have an adoring fan."

Malik swallowed hard, the words like wet cement in his throat. "You—put my husband in the hospital."

Fleece wasn't smiling anymore. His face hardened.

Malik pulled out a picture of Brett from his wallet and shoved it in Fleece's face. "This is my husband."

Fleece studied the photograph for a moment, then simpered coyly. "You're the cocksucker from Henley's Edge."

Malik shoved the photo back inside his wallet, pocketing it with love as if it were a precious gemstone. He could sense himself faltering, slowly inching away from Fleece as he continued to approach.

"I wondered if they'd rat me out," Fleece said.

"Who's they?" Malik ask, his voice quivering.

"Your neighbors. They want you faggots gone. Can't say I blame them. I'd sooner chew glass than have cocksuckers for neighbors."

Malik's fist tightened around the knife's handle. "You almost killed my husband."

Fleece chuckled. "Give me five seconds alone in a room with him. I'll finish the fucking job."

Just as Fleece glanced back at his gang near the bar's entrance, Malik swung the knife at him and missed. Fleece lunged at Malik, slamming his fist into the poor man's face again and again until Malik released the knife and it skidded beneath the car. Just as Malik was about to reach for the small handgun he had been concealing in his belt holster, Fleece swiped at the weapon and knocked it from his hands. Malik, too, was on the ground in a matter of seconds as Fleece overpowered him, pummeling him with all of his force. He felt the cartilage in his nose snap like tinder as Fleece punched him over and over again.

Out of his peripheral vision, Malik watched as others swarmed around him like gulls mobbing discarded food. He curled into a ball—trying to make himself as small as possible—as a boot slammed into his ribcage, another boot smashing his head. But it was to no avail—fists pummeling him until darkness crept at the corners of his vision and he began to see stars.

Just then, one of the other men ladled him from the ground and dumped his body into the car's open trunk. The last thing he remembered before oblivion swallowed him completely was the look on Fleece's face as he stared down at him—a look that seemed to tell Malik that his suffering was far from finished.

CHAPTER TWENTY

Ghost crawled out of the taxicab and told the driver to wait for him. Even though he had frequented the market for countless years, his visit today somehow felt different— as if he shouldn't be here, as if he were planning or participating in something truly unspeakable.

The little spirit tethered to his throat only seemed to make matters worse, hissing in his ear that everyone was watching him and serenading him with other falsities he knew couldn't possibly be true.

After all, why should anyone object to his presence at the market? It wasn't as if he were planning to steal something. Ghost was attentive to a fault. In fact, he was known to arrange disorganized cans and jars on supermarket shelves if he came across a mess.

After he swiped a small shopping cart from the store's entrance, he began to weave through the aisles until he came across the place where they stored the containers filled with honey. If he allowed his mind to wander too freely—if he contemplated the reason why he was actually here—he knew he might back down or contemplate his escape. As he stared at the jars of honey, the thoughts crept into his mind—thoughts of abandoning his post, thoughts of questioning his sanity for accepting such a ludicrous assignment in the first place.

He could scarcely believe the reason he had been sent to the grocery store in the first place—to collect honey so that one of the town's residents could offer his body as a sugary confection for God to consume. Ghost knew if he allowed himself to consider the lunacy of the situation too much, he might drive himself mad.

Just as he began to pile containers of honey into his cart, something in his peripheral vision caught him off guard. His eyes drifted further up the aisle and it was there he noticed Piper standing beside a large display of non-perishables. She stood there beside an older gentleman he assumed was her uncle. He watched as she coveted a large balloon in the shape of a giant heart with eyes and a smiling mouth.

He could hardly believe it. What were the chances he would see her again?

If he could somehow bring her back to Mr. Crowley's estate and reunite her with her mother, Gemma's trance might finally be broken. Of course, there was no way to prove this theory and it was entirely possible his plan wouldn't work, but he couldn't think of any other opportunity that might present itself to him so serendipitously.

He had to somehow lure Piper away from her guardian for the time being and return her to Mr. Crowley's place.

For a few minutes, Ghost stalked Piper and her uncle throughout the store and tried his best to remain out of sight. When the uncle swerved the cart down the bread aisle and Piper remained near the cartons of milk, Ghost realized it was his perfect chance.

He approached her gently, the same way an adult might approach a small, wild animal.

"Piper," he said. "Do you remember me?"

She immediately shrank from the sound of his voice, clutching her balloon a little tighter.

"It's OK," he said. "Don't be afraid. I'm the man with the magic stick. Remember? It grants wishes."

He watched as her face softened and she came to finally understand.

"Mommy was waiting for you to call her," Piper said.

Ghost exhaled; the reminder of poor Gemma was almost too excruciating to even comprehend.

"She said you were spineless," the little girl added. "And that you were a—pusillanimous—knuckle-walker."

Ghost smirked, realizing Gemma was probably right—after all, like many things, he had waited too long to make any semblance of a move.

"Would you like to see your mommy?" he asked her.

"You know where she is?"

Ghost nodded. "I can take you to her. But you can't tell anyone where you're going. Or where you've been when I bring you back. It has to be a secret. Do you understand?"

Piper nodded.

Without wasting another moment, Ghost took the little girl by the hand and led her down the canned goods aisle and out the sliding doors that led to the parking lot. The taxi was still waiting for him, idling near the curb.

Ghost pried open the door and helped Piper slide across the

seat. It was then he noticed the taxi driver looking at him queerly, a question begging to be answered.

"My niece," Ghost explained.

The driver nodded, seeming convinced and somewhat careless to probe even further.

After Ghost buckled the little girl's seatbelt, he gestured for the driver to drive on before anyone could possibly see them or report what he had done. Of course, he imagined by now the girl's poor uncle was in a frantic state, endlessly searching each aisle for his beloved niece only to be met with nothing. He felt a pang of guilt somewhere deep inside him—a little voice whispering to him that he was a monster and would always be one.

As the taxi peeled out of the supermarket parking lot, Ghost paid no attention to the red Subaru with newly replaced tires driven by the man with the dark goatee as it passed by their car. Why should he have noticed him or the tires? There was nothing unusual about him or the vehicle he was driving, despite the overly tinted windows. Why should he have suspected that there was something wrong, that there was something—someone—trapped in his car's trunk and pleading to be released?

After all, their paths had yet to cross in the way that the lives of all monsters are to eventually meet.

CHAPTER TWENTY-ONE

When the taxi arrived at Mr. Crowley's estate, Ghost asked the driver to wait for him while he took Piper inside. The little girl, towing her heart-shaped balloon as if it were the same spirit fettered to Ghost's throat, followed without comment as he led her into the massive entryway and closed the door behind her. It was as though he were sealing the entrance to an undisturbed Pharaoh's tomb.

That's exactly what the house was to Ghost, after all. A tomb.

Ducking into the parlor, he scanned the room for a sign of Mr. Crowley only to be met with an empty room. His eyes darted into the nearby dining room. Again, another spacious and empty room that would most likely still feel vacant even if it were filled with expensively dressed guests attending the most extravagant cotillion. He conceded there wasn't a single room in the house where a person could feel loved, wanted, less alone. The house seemed to take pleasure in the ache of the lonely soul, feeding off the alienated and the isolated.

Piper clutched her balloon a little tighter, apprehensive to move from where she was standing on the entryway's carpet.

"Where are we?" she asked.

"A place I probably shouldn't have brought you," he said, suddenly regretting his decision to kidnap her.

"You said mommy's here?"

"Yes," he said. "I'll take you to her."

Gently taking her hand, Ghost began to lead Piper down the cellar steps until they came to the basement. Everything was as he had left it—the rows of worshippers bowing, each seized in their own state of delirium, of private worship as they revered the glowing orb suspended in the room's corner. Guiding Piper through the worshippers as they made their daily prayers, their emphatic supplications to their deity, Ghost finally came upon Gemma near the front of the group.

He knelt beside her and brushed some of the hair from her face as she bowed to pray. Then, he looked to Piper, as if expecting a reaction from her and suddenly remembering she couldn't see.

"Your mom's right here," he told her, guiding the little girl's hands to touch Gemma's face.

Ghost watched in silence as Piper's fingers carefully mapped the entirety of her mother's face—from the lines on her forehead to the tiny mole beneath her chin.

"It's her," Piper exclaimed, throwing her arms around her mother.

Gemma received the embrace without comment, her lips forever moving with muted prayers. Piper shrank from her mother when she realized her love was to be ignored.

"Why won't she hug me?" the little girl asked.

Ghost tapped Gemma on the shoulder, gently purring in her ear. "Gemma, I brought your daughter to see you. She's right here."

But the zombified woman made no sign to suggest she had heard him. Her body was present, but her mind was very much elsewhere—lost somewhere deep in the glittering cosmos, floating there, perhaps waiting to be rescued or waiting for a certain absolution that had yet to be earned.

"What's wrong with my mommy?" Piper asked.

The question wounded Ghost. He moved away from Gemma and knelt in front of Piper.

"She's gone right now," he explained. "But she'll come back to you. I'll see to it."

"Where did she go?"

Ghost was unsure of what to say. How could he possibly explain what had happened to Gemma to her own daughter? Besides, who would believe him anyway?

"She's gone with God for the time being," he said.

"He took her away?"

"Yes. That's right," Ghost said. "But I'm doing everything I can to bring her back so she can be with you."

Piper seemed satisfied for the most part, her ice-cold glare thawing somewhat. She twirled the balloon string around her finger until her thumb was purple.

"Where is God?" she asked.

The little girl couldn't see, so Ghost knew she wouldn't believe him. Still, he said it anyway.

"He's here with us in this room right now," he told her. "Is there something you want to say to Him?"

Piper nodded. Then cleared some of the dampness from her eyes. "I would ask Him to please bring my mommy back. Let my mommy come home."

Ghost's eyes wandered to the corner where the walls met and observed the glowing orb of light. It merely swayed there against the wall, as unresponsive as the most primitive creature. He wanted nothing more than to sever the orb and let the light leak out like a bleeding egg yolk. Only then, he might feel peace, might feel a modicum of reconciliation knowing full well he had ended the existence of mankind's greatest threat: the Abrahamic God.

Gazing at Gemma once more, he knew that his plan hadn't worked. Not even the glorious sight of her own precious daughter would break the spell she had been placed under. He knew, once again, he had failed.

"I have to send you back home," he told her. "You promise you won't tell them where you were?"

Piper nodded. An unconvincing promise, but Ghost knew he would have to accept her word no matter what.

Guiding her back up the stairs and out to the car, he was almost at the doorway when he heard Mr. Crowley call to him upstairs.

"Is that you, home already?" the old man called out.

Ghost pushed Piper into the drawing room, hiding her behind the door in case Mr. Crowley possessed the ability to see around corners.

"Yes, they overcharged me at the market," Ghost shouted. "I'll be back in a few minutes."

"Don't take all day," Mr. Crowley begged him. "I need your help to prepare."

Ghost dragged Piper out from her hiding place and down the front steps toward the idling taxicab. Tossing her in the backseat and then climbing inside, he shut the door.

"Back to the supermarket, please," he ordered the driver.

When they arrived at the market, the parking area had been blocked off by several police cars with flickering lights. The taxi pulled onto the shoulder and slowed to a crawl until it parked.

"Remember what I told you," Ghost said to Piper.

She nodded. Then, she climbed out of the vehicle and began meander toward the store's front entrance, her little cane guiding the way.

Ghost didn't wait to see if the police ended up finding her wandering in the lot. He ordered the driver to head off immediately.

As he sat in the backseat, his mind worked over what Piper might tell them after she had been rescued. He wondered if she would tell her uncle of the man with the magic stick that grants wishes and how he had swept her away to a magical home where God was kept in the cellar. He knew for a fact it was a secret that could not be kept. He understood that. But then again, who would believe her?

He wasn't worried about that in the least. All he could think of was Gemma—saving her from a terrible fate and returning her to her beloved daughter. He realized every moment he wasted away from the house and beginning the ritual was a detriment to Gemma and the other poor souls trapped in the basement. He knew he had to find a way to set them free, no matter the cost.

PART FOUR

AN INVENTION OF SKIN

"The wound is the place where the Light enters you."
—Rumi

CHAPTER TWENTY-TWO

Blurred specks of light flickered at the corners of Malik's vision as soon as his eyelids fluttered open. It pained him to swallow, as if his throat were scorched with ash and salt. His head throbbed, vision pulsing in and out of focus whenever he stirred. It was then he realized his arms and legs were bound with cables to bedposts. His mouth—gagged with socks and covered with duct tape.

His eyes scanned the room—from the radiator near the drape-covered window to the television stand piled with opened candy wrappers and takeout cartons. He noticed a man dressed in dark clothing milling about near the room's entrance, peering through the blinds and out into the motel parking lot. Immediately he recognized him—one of the men that had been standing in front of the Stateline Bar. Yes, that's precisely where he had seen him. What else had he remembered?

He searched his mind for meaning, for how he had ended up here. He could recall nothing. The last thing he remembered was darkness eating away at his vision until he was floating somewhere, being carried by invisible arms toward a bright white light before being pulled away at the last moment.

He made eye contact with the man standing beside the motel room door. At first, his eyes pleaded with him—silently begging to be released the way an animal might when caught in a steel trap. But Malik quickly realized this man had no intention of helping him. It was evident in the way he looked at him—the same way a fisherman regards a fish with a hook speared through its jaw.

"Hey, Saint," the man called out. "He's up."

The bathroom door swung open, revealing Fleece as he stood there without a shirt and zipping up his fly.

He was a specimen of manhood. Malik recognized that. Perhaps once he might have lusted after him. Perhaps once he might have invented scenarios of the two of them together, but not now. Not after knowing what he had done—even worse, what his eyes told him he was planning to do.

"Sleeping beauty," Fleece said to Malik. "So glad you're well rested."

Malik strained to speak, but he remained gagged.

"Where am I?" he blurted from beneath the gag set in his mouth.

"Where are you?" Fleece laughed. "You're at the party, man. And you're our special party favor."

Malik swallowed hard, a dull ache burning in the pit of his throat.

His eyes widened when he saw Fleece pull out a small pocketknife from his jeans, the blade glinting at him in the light.

The motel door room opened, and another one of Fleece's gang members entered. This one, dressed in black tactical military gear and chewing on a Twizzler.

"Did I miss it?" he asked as he closed the door behind him.

"You're just in time," Fleece said, approaching Malik on the bed with the pocketknife.

Malik could do nothing but squirm against the restraints, making muffled screams against the gag. Fleece knelt beside him, unbuttoning Malik's shirt and exposing his naked chest.

"When I was a boy, I grew up on a farm with my grandparents," Fleece explained, admiring the tiny blade in his hands. "One of my favorite things to do was brand the livestock. But my grandfather never let me do it. I guess he thought I was too zealous. You'll forgive me if I get too excited, won't you?"

Malik shook his head, begging him to stop. Fleece ignored him, ordering his men to hold his arms and legs down so that he could go to work. Straddling Malik's body, Fleece pressed the edge of the knife down against Malik's chest until a line of blood sprouted and crept there. Malik winced, Fleece's knife going up and down his chest—his skin heating beneath the blade as he went about his work. He prayed for numbness, but instead he felt every slash, every slit, every tear as more of his blood flowered from the knife's edge until his chest was dark and flooded with red.

When Fleece had finished his labor, he wiped the blood from Malik's chest and revealed his work—the word "FAG" had been carved into the center of Malik's chest, the places where his skin had been parted to build the curve of each letter resembled that of a gruesome patchwork quilt.

Malik's eyes watered, the word claiming him and dragging him further down into his own private despair where he longed to hide from Fleece and the rest of his gang. The word had followed him since he was very small and now it was forever a part of him—a mark on his body, a wound that would scab over and heal but would always be there no matter what. It wasn't long before Fleece wrenched him from his beloved hiding spot, yanking him out like a rotted weed and discarding him there as if he were nothing more than a tattered, old towel.

"Undo his arms and legs," Fleece ordered, climbing off Malik's body.

His followers looked at one another, bewildered.

"Now," he demanded.

The two men unwrapped the wires from Malik's legs and tore off his shoes. This was his moment. It wasn't much, but perhaps if he kicked hard enough, he might be able to tear himself free.

As soon as they slid the wires from his ankles, Malik thrashed and kicked one of the men in the face. Just as he was about to wrench one of the wires pulling on his arm, Fleece climbed on top of Malik once more and held him down.

"You still have some fight left in you, I see," Fleece said, visibly pleased as he unwrapped the cables binding both of Malik's arms. "Good. I want you to feel everything."

As Malik squirmed helplessly, Fleece flipped his body over and yanked down his pants until his ass was fully exposed. Malik screamed, the gag working its way deeper down his throat until he almost choked, as he sensed Fleece straddle him once more. Malik felt Fleece unzip his pants and press himself against his body.

Without warning, Fleece slammed himself against Malik so forcefully that Malik wondered if he had shoved a razorblade inside his intestines—the agony working its way through his viscera until it clawed its way out through his muffled mouth in a soft scream that no one could hear.

There was nothing that Malik could do but wait for it to be over.

After all, from this moment forward, his body no longer belonged to him. It belonged to Fleece. To Malik, Fleece was now God. He prayed quietly that he'd be a merciful one.

However, there was something in the way that Fleece ordered the other men in the room to begin to undress that told Malik he wouldn't be.

CHAPTER TWENTY-THREE

Ghost wasn't sure what to expect when he entered the drawing room that evening. All of the furniture had been crammed into the corners of the room and draped with white linen. Mr. Crowley was already waiting for him when he arrived, the old man eyeing him with a dangerous invitation—a warning that he would be remorseful if he did not obey.

Of course, Ghost was prepared to submit. After all, Mr. Crowley had promised him that the ritual would set Gemma and the others free. Regardless, he couldn't be certain what the old man had prepared, what he had expected from him and, even worse, what he had wanted him to do in exchange for their freedom.

In the few moments they had been alone in one another's company, Ghost had noticed there was a profound sense of longing in Mr. Crowley's voice when he spoke to him—the gentle way a forlorn lover might speak when addressing their dying betrothed. Ghost couldn't help but wonder if the old man fancied him, if he indulged in fantasies too obscene to even mention—both of their bodies sweating and naked, tangled like snakes coiled in a nest.

Ghost hadn't been involved with another man before his relationship with Hailey and although part of him was curious to return to the companionship often found in coupling with the same sex, he knew he felt no attraction whatsoever to Mr. Crowley. Even his supernatural powers, as tempting and beguiling as they were, left him uninspired to pursue even a physical relationship with him.

Despite all this, he couldn't help but wonder if Mr. Crowley was planning something, if this entire scenario was an excuse to undress him and expose him to his most dangerous desires.

As soon as Ghost entered the room, he noticed the old man carrying a large satchel. Mr. Crowley was dressed in an expensive looking burgundy-colored satin bathrobe that dragged on the floor like a bridal train when he walked.

"Mr. Everling," the old man said, bowing to greet him. "Please remove your robe and lie down."

Ghost shifted uncomfortably, tugging on the collar of the robe Mr. Crowley had ordered him to wear tighter against his throat. The little spirit at his ear coiled inside, hissing.

"He's going to fuck the life out of you," the tiny wraith whistled. "You're just meat to him."

Ghost cleared the catch in his throat. "Undress?" he asked Mr. Crowley.

"The ritual is to begin and end with purity, dear boy," Mr. Crowley explained. "We want things done properly, don't we?"

Of course, Ghost could have protested further. But something deep inside him—a tiny spring of metal heating and uncoiling at the old man's command—seemed to compel him to remove his robe until he was fully naked. He stood there for a moment, his body completely exposed, as Mr. Crowley regarded him with desirous eyes. It wasn't necessarily a lecherous desire, but rather the way some older men regard younger men and their vitality that no longer belongs to them. Mr. Crowley peeled his bathrobe from him, revealing himself until he was completely naked too.

There was nothing unattractive about the old man. In fact, Ghost reasoned that there was a semblance of liveliness hiding somewhere beneath the old man's sagging pectorals or his hairless groin. Ghost's eyes couldn't help but be drawn to a pair of lesions—dark patches of skin as red as wine—just above the old man's abdominals. Mr. Crowley seemed to notice his staring, his hand moving to cover them as if out of embarrassment.

After they stood there for a few moments, silently comparing one another and growing accustomed to the unease of each other's nakedness, Mr. Crowley gestured for Ghost to move to the center of the space.

"Please," he said. "Won't you lie down?"

Ghost hesitated. "And you'll do what?"

"My dear boy, this ritual won't work if you don't trust me implicitly," Mr. Crowley explained, retrieving the satchel and untying it. "Now, please. Won't you?"

Although he remained on guard—protecting himself as best he could while still naked—Ghost moved to the center of the room and knelt until his body was pressed against the floor. Visibly satisfied with his compliance, Mr. Crowley flipped the satchel upside down and began to scatter sand across the floor. Circling Ghost, Mr. Crowley poured sand out until the satchel was empty.

Remaining inside the circle of sand he had drawn around Ghost's naked body, Mr. Crowley began to recite a prayer in Latin. Ghost watched in silence as the old man circled him, recounting his petition. The floor seemed to quiver as Mr. Crowley spoke in his dead language, the nearby candlelight flickering and casting the old man's giant silhouette against the wall like shadow puppetry.

Ghost shuddered. The floor seemed to move beneath him, the floorboards beginning to gently clap as if in response to Mr. Crowley's prayer.

The old man swiped a nearby knife and brandished it in front of Ghost the same way a cleric might flourish a holy relic. Ghost squirmed, about to leap from the ground when he realized he could not move—it was as if a concrete weight had been piled on his chest. He struggled against the invisible weight, calling out to Mr. Crowley to stop the ritual. But the old man would not listen. He was already pressing the knife against the palm of his hand, a thin wire of blood curling there. There was nothing Ghost could do but watch as Mr. Crowley chanted in Latin and held his blood-soaked palm over his face.

Ghost winced, the old man's blood dripping on his forehead. It wasn't long before Ghost's face was spattered with red.

"What the fuck are you doing?" he shouted at him, leaping from the floor, and wiping the blood from his face. "You sick fuck."

Mr. Crowley, finally severed from his trance, looked at Ghost with bewilderment. "You almost ruined the ritual."

"I almost swallowed your blood, you piece of shit," Ghost said. "You're disgusting."

"The ritual's not complete," the old man warned him. "We still have to finish it."

But Ghost was already across the threshold of sand and snatching his robe from the ground, heading for the door. "I'm not finishing anything. I'm done with this. I'm going to the police."

"You can't. Once the ritual has started it needs to be finished," Mr. Crowley said, shadowing him. "I told you that you need to trust me."

"Trust you? You're a fucking monster."

"I can make it so that you're rewarded with more than money when we're finished, dear boy," Mr. Crowley said.

But Ghost wasn't convinced. "I'm done. I'm not making any more deals with you."

"He can bring Hailey back," Mr. Crowley said.

Ghost froze for a moment, his dead wife's name pulsing through him like an electrical current.

"How do you—know her name?" he asked him.

Mr. Crowley simpered coyly. "You underestimate me, dear boy. You don't think I know about what you most desperately want? What did I say about the art of salesmanship? It's about anticipating, knowing a person's true needs."

Ghost felt unclean, as if he could sense Mr. Crowley crawling around inside him, rummaging through his thoughts and overturning stacks of memories until he came upon the one thing that mattered most to Ghost—his sweet Hailey. He knew he should leave, but a curious part of him begged to know the answer to a question that needed to be asked.

"How could He bring her back?" he asked.

Mr. Crowley smiled, as if pleased with Ghost's inquisitiveness. "I can alter the ritual in our favor, dear boy. He can undo what's been done. I can order Him to bring her back to you."

181

Ghost thought for a moment, glimpses of Hailey—the lovely young woman she once was, the beauty she once possessed—blinking through his mind like grainy photographs displayed on an antique film projector.

"You're certain He will?" Ghost asked him quietly.

"Trust me, dear boy," the old man said. "You'll get her back."

Ghost was quiet, as if Mr. Crowley had snatched his tongue by the very root. He thought for a moment. What could he possibly say? He wanted Hailey back most of all. Life was unbearable without her. This could be his chance to change everything.

"How do we finish the ritual?" he asked the old man.

Mr. Crowley flashed a grin at him. Then, with a flick of his wrist, the old man commanded the beads of blood smeared along Ghost's forehead to form the shape of a small cross. When he was finished and satisfied with his work, Mr. Crowley completed the prayer in Latin.

"Amen," he whispered, pushing his thumb against Ghost's forehead and wiping the blood away until Ghost was clean once more.

The entire house trembled—the floorboards creaking, the walls quivering as if they were gelatin. A deep, guttural moan came rising up from beneath the floor and filled the room for a moment before the sound dimmed to a mere whisper.

Ghost looked at Mr. Crowley, expecting an explanation.

"It begins," the old man said.

CHAPTER TWENTY-FOUR

The following morning, Ghost found Mr. Crowley waiting for him in the dining room.

"Do you always sleep so late?" Mr. Crowley asked. "Pleasant dreams, I imagine?"

Quite the contrary. Ghost had been up for most of the night, his sheets drenched in sweat—too fearful to return to sleep and face the onslaught of unpleasant thoughts that seemed to tirelessly circle in his mind—dreams involving Mr. Crowley.

Of course, Ghost had quietly thanked God that their first night of the ritual had ended early and that they had retired to their separate rooms without matters becoming physical. Still, there was something beguiling about Mr. Crowley—something about him that had yet to be revealed to Ghost. It didn't matter that Ghost had seen his most private parts—there was something hidden in a deep grotto inside the old man like an oasis tucked away in the hills of a sand swept desert: something Ghost was determined to find and pluck out from him.

"I'm afraid not," Ghost said. "I had—strange dreams all night."

"They were vivid?" the old man asked.

"Yes."

"Perhaps you'd care to tell me?"

Ghost wasn't sure. Of course, sharing his naked body with the old man was one thing, but revealing the privacy of his dreams—that was a level of intimacy he hadn't approached since Hailey had passed. In fact, one of his favorite things to do in the morning was make her breakfast and narrate to her the dreams he could remember from the night before. In turn, she would share hers as well. But to share his most private, most revealing thoughts with Mr. Crowley? He thought the mere act of intercourse would be far less probing and maybe even more preferable.

Regardless, he let his guard down for a moment and complied.

"I dreamt of you actually," Ghost said. "I dreamt the two of us were—"

But his voice trailed off, unsure how to delicately say it.

"Fucking like wild animals?" Mr. Crowley asked.

Ghost blushed, nodding.

"Good," the old man said, spooning some fruit onto Ghost's plate.

Good? Ghost couldn't see exactly what was so good about it. In his dreams, Mr. Crowley had mounted him like a feral creature in heat—stabbing his entrails until they were swollen red and bleeding. It hadn't been like the lovemaking he had cherished and grown accustomed to with Hailey—the gentle passion, the deep affection. Instead, it had been rough and frightening—as if Mr. Crowley wanted to reach up inside him and rip out his bloody, beating heart until he could squeeze it in his hands.

"That means the ritual's working, dear boy," Mr. Crowley explained, passing a piece of burnt toast to him.

Ghost accepted the bread without comment.

It was then he noticed another dark lesion on Mr. Crowley's throat. The old man seemed to notice his staring, pulling his eyes away and pouring a cup of tea.

Should he ask him? Ghost wondered. After all, they had been naked together—they should have no secrets from one another.

"I was wondering," Ghost began, then stopped.

The words seemed too forced, too calculated. He wondered what to say.

"I mean, I couldn't help but notice," Ghost said, gesturing to the lesion on Mr. Crowley's throat. "When we were—together—last night."

Mr. Crowley frowned, as if he had been dreading the question. "You don't want to hear about an old man's sickness."

The word pierced through Ghost—"sickness." He knew exactly what it was but dared not name it. It was the same disease that his father wished upon him when he finally came out years ago—the very last thing his father had ever said to him.

"But your powers," Ghost said. "Couldn't you—?"

"I've tried," the old man said. "I can't."

Ghost watched as Mr. Crowley lowered his head for a moment, visibly bruised by the reminder of his disease. He no longer resembled the strong, charismatic charmer that Ghost had come to know. Instead, he was an epitaph of his former self, an inscription on a tombstone—quiet and reflective.

"My husband gave it to me," Mr. Crowley explained. "Picked it up from a whore he slept with on a business trip to Seattle. Doesn't make the condition any more bearable, but at least I know."

Ghost said nothing, his eyes fixed on Mr. Crowley as he spoke.

"He gave it to me and then he left," Mr. Crowley said. "Said he couldn't live with the reminder of what he had done to me every day."

Mr. Crowley resembled something so small—a miniature artifact you might find at an excavation site or a tiny relic from a human body back when Ancient Egyptians once placed the organs of their dead in small canopic jars.

"It just goes to show you can create something and then abandon it," Mr. Crowley said before rising from his chair and excusing himself from the dining room.

Ghost sat there alone for a moment. The old man was right. After all, that's exactly what God had done to him—gave him the gift of Hailey and then took his precious love away. Remembering Mr. Crowley's promise, he knew he had a duty to finish the ritual. Not only would he be saving Gemma and the others, but he would be reunited with his love.

He'd be damned before he let her slip away again.

CHAPTER TWENTY-FIVE

Malik had been drifting in and out of consciousness when Fleece finally returned to the motel room. Fleece carried a large rucksack he had slung over his shoulder, white powder smearing his upper lip from something he had snorted while in his car. His men had wrapped a towel around Malik's bare bottom to stop some of the bleeding from the work they had done on him— the hours they had spent passing him around as if he were lifeless, a submissive corpse eager to satisfy their most perverted amusements.

Numbness had finally claimed him, and he felt nothing when they flipped him on his backside and dressed him, securing his arms and legs with rope and gagging him once more. There were moments— few and far between—when he could have retaliated if he'd had the strength. There were missed opportunities to escape, moments when he could have easily overcome his assailants while Fleece was gone. These moments seemed to come and go as Malik's body was present, but his spirit was very much elsewhere—his desire to escape, even his will to live seemed to abandon him the very moment Fleece and his men had defiled him. He had retreated into some quiet den deep inside himself, a place where not even Fleece and his scrupulous gaze could follow.

"What the fuck is this?" Fleece asked, gesturing to the blood-soaked towel wrapped around Malik's underside. "Are you more concerned about making him comfortable?"

"He wouldn't stop bleeding," one of the men answered. "It was getting everywhere."

"Let him bleed out," another one responded, twisting open a candy wrapper.

Fleece seemed to recognize the damage they had done in such a short amount of time—Malik's blood and excrement spattered across the bedsheets, more blood pooling there by the minute.

"No, he's right," he said. "We need a cleaner workspace."

Then his eyes drifted to the bathroom doorway.

"Move him to the tub," Fleece demanded, pinching a cigarette between his fingers and lighting it with a match. "We'll finish working on him in there."

Fleece's men immediately grabbed hold of Malik, securing his arms and legs with ropes, and ferried him to the bathroom. Peeling back the shower curtain, they loaded him in and dropped him in the bathtub. Malik could have resisted, could have spit at them or struggled against their bondage—but he remained lost somewhere deep inside himself, unable to answer when his determination called to him. It was as if Fleece and his men had done more than merely broke his spirit; they had destroyed him without killing him.

"Leave the two of us alone," Fleece ordered, taking another drag from his cigarette.

His men obeyed, slipping out of the bathroom and closing the door once they had left.

Malik watched, his eyelids heavy, as Fleece sauntered over to the bathroom vanity beside the toilet. He watched as Fleece inspected his reflection, combing his dark hair until it was set just right. Malik had to admit that Fleece's hair was glorious—as black as a raven's wings and falling just past his shoulders in beautiful curls. He felt strange ogling his captor, silently praising his beauty as if optimistic that his praise might spare him in the end. Though he was hopeful, in his heart Malik knew it wouldn't work. He knew that his imprisoner was a monster and that he wouldn't be satisfied until Malik's body was a grotesque puzzle of human anatomy that nobody could solve.

Fleece seemed to notice Malik was staring at his reflection and they made intense eye contact.

"You know, I prefer you to your husband," Fleece said, turning toward Malik and approaching him. "You don't beg for your life. You don't make the mistake of embarrassing yourself. Not like that little spineless fuck of yours we put in the hospital."

Malik's mind went to Brett—thoughts of him as he was told the news that his husband had perished, how he might go weak at the knees and sob in the arms of officers, how he might be asked to identify the body. If they even found his body, that is.

"He begged me to let him live," Fleece said, kneeling beside Malik. "Begged me not to kill him."

Fleece pushed the end of his cigarette into Malik's forehead. Malik moaned in agony, the gag working its way further into his mouth until he nearly retched at the soreness.

"How could I in good conscience let a God-hating faggot live?" Fleece asked, pulling out a switchblade from his rucksack.

Malik said nothing. He merely stared at the ceiling and began counting tiles, waiting for it to be over—for darkness to claim him once more and perhaps this time for good.

Fleece poked him with the switchblade. "Hey. Do you know why I hate your kind so fucking much? Do you know why I was too glad to help your neighbors when they came to me?"

Malik closed his eyes, tears webbing in the corners.

"When I was little, I went into the woods to play with my friend Tommy," Fleece explained, gliding the knife across Malik's throat. "Just when we were about to head back, a man stopped us. Came out of nowhere. 'You're both in big trouble,' he said. 'You're not supposed to be here. Don't you know that?'"

Malik watched in silence as Fleece's face hardened at the memory.

"So, he ordered Tommy and I to undress. Said he wanted to see us—touch each other—while he took pictures with his camera," Fleece said. "When we were finished, he told us that if we ever told anyone what we had done, he'd show those pictures to our parents."

Malik could hear Fleece's voice shuddering slightly with a fear-filled tremor, as if he were still that scared little boy—as if he still lived in constant fear of seeing those photographs, as if they owned him to this very day and he were a mere puppet.

Although he struggled to murmur something beneath the gag, Malik could barely hold his head up. When Fleece noticed his dozing, he pressed the knife harder against his throat.

"Tommy and I never spoke about what we did that day. Never told anyone about the man we saw or what we had done together," Fleece said. "But it got the better of him because two years later, he put a gun in his mouth and pulled the trigger. All because of a faggot."

Malik tried to speak to him with his eyes, tried to offer a look of sympathy to inform him that he doesn't have to be afraid anymore—that he doesn't have to live in fear and, more importantly, that Malik and his community are not monsters. But Fleece seemed to ignore the peace offering almost immediately, tapping Malik with the edge of the knife.

"I'm stopping you before you have a chance to ruin some other child's life," Fleece said, his voice quivering as if he were trying to convince himself.

Malik's eyes begged him. If there was a semblance of humanity remaining inside Fleece, Malik searched for it. But it was no use. Fleece regarded him with such hatred—such unimaginable disgust and loathing.

Fleece softened. Malik could see the scared child residing inside the poor man—youth extinguished and robbed before its proper time. He felt sorry for him and Malik wondered if Fleece might let him go, might set him free and let him live with the agony of what had been done to him.

But that longing was quickly dashed as Fleece raised the switchblade and brought it down heavy into Malik's gut. Malik winced, the knife going deep inside him and twisting like a corkscrew. He sensed his stomach curl, the knife slipping out and then being brought down again into his armpit. Malik gagged at the pain, numbness abandoning him so that he could feel the intensity of each stab. Finally, in a blow that would decide the matter, Fleece pushed the switchblade into Malik's face.

Vision blurred and dimmed from Malik's right eye until darkness was his permanent companion. He sensed his body twitch gently as Fleece continued to slash him, blood sprinkling his face as his assailant went about his gruesome labor.

There came a moment when Malik was no longer present—when Fleece's forceful stabs were the gentle touches of a loving parent or a caregiver, when his blood was a river that would carry him to a wondrous land far away where pain could no longer follow, and he was finally free.

CHAPTER TWENTY-SIX

Ghost dreaded the invitation to another ritual.

He arrived to find the nearly overflowing bathtub surrounded with candles, Mr. Crowley loitering nearby in his familiar burgundy-colored satin bathrobe. Drawn in black sand at the center of the bathroom's tiled floor was a strange shape—something not unlike an Ancient Egyptian hieroglyph.

"Welcome, dear boy," the old man said as Ghost entered the room. "This is one of the most crucial parts of the ritual so that we both get what we want."

Of course, he would say that, Ghost conceded. The old man still yearned for Ghost's compliance and never seemed satisfied.

"Please remove your robe," Mr. Crowley ordered, removing his.

Ghost complied, peeling off his bathrobe and standing naked in front of the old man once again.

"Get into the bathtub," the old man said.

Ghost hesitated slightly, but it wasn't long before he had climbed into the tub and was curled inside as warm bath water lapped against his naked skin.

"Can you hold your breath, dear boy?" Mr. Crowley asked, kneeling beside the bathtub.

Ghost nodded. He had loved to swim in his younger days but hadn't swum since Hailey had passed.

"You'll have to go under and hold your breath while I recite the prayer," Mr. Crowley explained. "It's imperative you stay under until I'm finished."

Ghost nodded again, understanding. He drew in a deep breath and then lowered himself beneath the surface until he was fully submerged. Closing his eyes, he floated there and listened to the dim hum of Mr. Crowley's voice as he recited another prayer in Latin. As he hovered beneath water, he thought of his beloved Hailey—what he would say to her if Mr. Crowley made good on his promise, what they might do the moment they saw one another. He loathed himself for admitting it—but he had forgotten her smell. Something he once savored every day was now lost to him. But hopefully not for long. If Mr. Crowley was speaking the truth, she would return to him, and things would be as they were before.

As seconds turned to minutes, Ghost pried open his eyes beneath water and searched for a sight of Mr. Crowley beyond the blurred screen of bath water. He could find nothing. Just as he was about to lift himself out of the tub, a hand came down and held him down beneath the water—keeping him there as if hoping he might drown. Ghost thrashed under the pressure, limbs flailing helplessly as water fountained from the tub. Everything slowed to a hypnotic pulse, a shimmering screen of water circling Ghost while he clawed at the surface. Water began to fill his lungs and light filled his periphery until it was snatched away and Mr. Crowley dragged him out of the tub and spread his naked body out against the tiled floor.

Ghost shivered and coughed, his body spasming as Mr. Crowley draped a blanket over him to dry him off.

"What—the fuck were you doing?" he shouted at the old man.

Mr. Crowley held a finger to his lips. "Wait. It's not finished yet."

With a grand flourish, the old man cast his eyes heavenward. "Amen," he said.

The room began to tremble—the house quivering as if held in the palm of a livid giant. Ghost clung to the rim of the bathtub for support while Mr. Crowley braced himself against the sink. The tiled floor spilt apart—a giant crack spiderwebbing across the floor and splitting one of the walls in two as if they were made of kindling.

After a steady throbbing, the house began to settle into itself—sound vacuumed from the room and any hint of further destruction was now very much gone for the time being.

Ghost and the old man looked at one another, bewildered and wondering if the worst was behind them.

"It worked," Mr. Crowley said.

"How can you tell?"

The old man swiped his bathrobe from the floor and dressed before running out of the bathroom.

Ghost dressed quickly and followed the old man down the stairs and deep into the cellar where they finally came upon the worshippers. Only this time the rows of people were not bathed in a heavenly glow. Instead, the room was dimly lit—a gentle light emanating from the corner where the giant orb once hung. It was then that Ghost and Mr. Crowley saw it—the vague outline of a human body seared into the concrete cellar wall, the edges of the shape smoldering as if freshly burned.

The arms and legs of the shape were elongated, serpentine-almost with small glowing tendrils like roots blooming from each of its impossibly long fingers. Fixed in the center of the vaguely human shape—presumably where its heart was rooted—was a single flame that flickered and seethed.

"What is it?" Ghost asked, hesitant to approach the strange shape.

"It's changing Him," Mr. Crowley explained.

"Into what?"

"Preparing to return Him to heaven," he replied.

But Ghost wasn't convinced.

The shape in the wall resembled the remnants of some foul thing vaporized in a nuclear blast—something caught in the moment of impact, something that continued to exist in a state of suffering even though its time had already come. Its very presence seemed impossible—its extremities as thin as threads and fuming with smoke, its ornate, fully exposed circulatory system etched into the concrete and cycling furiously to keep the thing in a precious state of living.

If you could even call it living.

Ghost couldn't help but wonder if the God Mr. Crowley had conjured could feel pain, if He endured in anguish and could do nothing but wait for the next ritual to be completed so that He could be spared of His misery. Whatever the case may be, Ghost couldn't help but yearn for the moment when God would be completely at his mercy and subject to his most capricious whims. Only then would Ghost feel satisfied.

CHAPTER TWENTY-SEVEN

Malik pretended to be dead.

Although it was apparent to him that with the amount of blood he had already lost and would keep losing, death was not far and would be making its presence known to him very soon. After all, Fleece had gone to town on his poor body with the switchblade. How Malik had survived was an absolute miracle—a marvel he had hoped to keep from his captors for as long as possible.

He knew he couldn't overpower them, couldn't plan a surprise attack on the group of men. He was far too weak. The only thing he could do was wait for the perfect moment—when they let their guards down or when he knew they couldn't do any further harm to him. Of course, he was uncertain when and even if that moment would ever come.

What other monstrous things could they do to him? They had already done the worst—something Malik would have to live with for the rest of his life. If he survived, that was.

After Fleece and his men had scrubbed the bathtub and cleaned the bedsheets soaked with Malik's blood, they wrapped his body in the shower curtain. He laid there without movement as they swaddled him, his eyes firmly shut.

"Alright. Bring him out to the car," Fleece ordered his men.

Shoveling his limp body off the ground, Fleece's cronies hauled Malik from the bathroom floor and ushered him out of the motel room toward the car idling nearby. They dumped his body in the trunk and slammed the lid shut, darkness devouring him whole as if he had been swallowed by a leviathan—some underwater titan that would make mincemeat of his assailants. If only he possessed the power, he thought. If only he could conjure some legendary creature to devour his attackers and spare him any further anguish.

It wasn't long after he heard the car's engine rev that he sensed himself rolling to one side of the trunk as the car tore out of the motel parking lot. Malik continued to slip in and out of consciousness—darkness when he closed his eyes, darkness when he opened them. He wouldn't allow himself to die inside a car trunk. There were other far more dignified places where the authorities could find his body. This was certainly not one of them.

After what felt like hours, he sensed the car slow to a crawl and the engine shut off. His ears pinned at the noise of approaching footsteps. The lid to the trunk flew open, revealing Fleece and his men once more. They grabbed Malik's body and ladled him from the trunk, hauling him out and onto the shoulder of the road where they had parked the vehicle.

"Just dump him here," Fleece said to his men.

"Like this?" one of them asked, concerned.

"I want them to find him," Fleece said, kicking Malik's body in the gut one final time.

Malik sensed Fleece's men grab hold of his body. For a moment, he felt swaddled as if he were a child. The care they took with him suddenly came to a halt as they kicked his body down a ravine on the side of the road, little twigs and branches exploding as Malik's limp body careened down the embankment and landed face-first in a small thicket of ferns.

One of the men hollered with joy, praising their handiwork. Another pulled down his pants and began to urinate, sprinkling Malik's body with a geyser until he was finished.

"Back in the car, cocksuckers," Fleece ordered his men. "You want us to get caught?"

Malik faintly heard the sound of Fleece and his men retreat to their vehicle, the car's tires squealing like frightened livestock as they peeled off and down the road. When Malik was certain they had left, he opened the shower curtain and crawled out from within. Although it pained him to move, he knew he had to or else he'd die here.

It certainly wasn't an unpleasant place to die, however. His eyes drifted up, giant sycamores and elms towering above him. Rainwater dotted his face from a passing thunderstorm. Wind gently rustled him with the same faintness and tenderness of an adoring mother's touch.

He knew if he wanted to survive, he had to move from where he was. Nobody would ever find him in a deep ravine on the side of a deserted backroad. Of course, he had hoped that by now they might be looking for him, but he couldn't bank on that fact right now.

With trembling hands, he clawed his way up the embankment—his gut paining him from where Fleece had stabbed him—until he was at the summit. Dragging himself through the dirt and the mud, he came to the road and rested there for a moment. He waited, pressing his ear against the pavement and straining to listen for the sound of an approaching car. Nothing.

Straightening himself on quivering legs, he rose to his knees and steadied his breathing as he stood there on the side of the road. He wondered what kind of abomination he must resemble—his face rusted brown with dried blood, his hair greased and matted with the same. His appearance was the least of his worries right now, however. As he glanced down at his stomach, he noticed a dark stain blooming in the center of his abdominals from where Fleece had twisted the switchblade. He winced, applying pressure there as more blood leaked out and dyed his shirt red.

Staggering down the single lane roadway, Malik limped for what felt like miles. Each step—a revocation of what Fleece and his men had done. Each breath he took—a reminder that he was still very much alive and would be as long as he continued to fight. Every bead of blood that pattered behind him in a trail—a reminder of where he had once been and where he would never return.

It wasn't long before he came upon a driveway. Figuring a house was nearby, a place where he could call for help, he began limping down the driveway. The road stretched for what seemed like miles before he came upon a clearing tucked away and a giant house dwarfing the neighboring tree line. The home—a behemoth of a manor, a place only written about in bloodless fables whispered to precious children at bedtime.

There, parked in front of the giant house, was a black Rolls-Royce—a chariot fit for a God.

Malik limped past the vehicle and toward the front stairs. He winced as he climbed each step—as if he were ascending, as if he were arriving at the very precipice that separates Heaven from Hell.

PART FIVE

HYMNS FOR A DECAYING GOD

"All I have seen teaches me to trust the Creator for all
I have not seen."

—Ralph Waldo Emerson

CHAPTER TWENTY-EIGHT

Even though Ghost had once yearned for God's destruction—desired the very moment when his supposedly great Creator would capsize from greatness—there was something unbearable about what he and Mr. Crowley were doing to Him.

God resembled a mere beggar caught in the exquisite throes of agony—the carcass of a wretched panhandler fated to be spooned from the street after death and dumped into a mass grave on the outskirts of a foreign city.

"We have an opportunity to complete the ritual now, dear boy," Mr. Crowley said. "We mustn't wait."

"Here?" Ghost asked, looking around the cellar at the rows of worshippers as if thinking one of them might raise a hand to object. "Right now?"

"I'm afraid we'll misplace the powers already very much at work if we don't seize this opportunity immediately," the old man explained.

Ghost leaned against his cane for support. Of course, he wanted more than anything to finish the ritual and to save Gemma. But something moved inside Ghost—something that whispered to him that this was all very wrong.

"If this is going to work, I need you to offer me the very last of your resistance, dear boy," Mr. Crowley demanded. "I know you've been hiding it from me."

Ghost conceded that perhaps he was right. Ghost had yet to fully let his guard down when around the old man. Even when he was naked, he kept a part of himself quartered away—a secret place deep inside him which he had yet to decay.

Mr. Crowley held out his hands for Ghost to take.

Although reluctant, Ghost placed his hands in the old man's. He shuddered at his touch, as if a power beyond his comprehension were working its way through him—an electrical current passing from one body to another, a secret language only their bodies seemed to be able to understand.

Mr. Crowley circled Ghost and seemed to take inventory of his handiwork, to challenge him with a warning if anything else was left undisturbed.

"Very good, dear boy," Mr. Crowley said, rubbing Ghost's shoulders.

The little spirit tethered to Ghost's throat swatted at the old man, hissing.

"Now, I'd like you to lay down on the floor," Mr. Crowley said, undressing from his robe. "I'll begin with a prayer. I want you to let yourself go and trust in me, dear boy."

Second nature to him by now, Ghost removed his robe, leaned his cane against the wall, and spread himself out on the ground. Mr. Crowley took a few steps toward him, hovering over Ghost's body and regarding him with the loving eyes of a father—the eyes of a father Ghost had never had. Ghost squirmed, awkwardly covering his manhood as Mr. Crowley hovered above him and prayed in Latin.

Ghost sensed his body loosen and begin to move on its own as if it had been silently commanded to do so. Glancing down, he noticed the floor pulling further and further away from him until he was floating in mid-air. He squirmed like an earthworm impaled on a fishing hook, dangling there as if his body were being held by an illusionist's invisible string.

"Wait," he said, floating further up into the air as the cellar's ceiling approached. "What is this—?"

But Mr. Crowley ignored him, the sounds of his prayers intensifying.

Ghost's eyes widened when he noticed Mr. Crowley command his cane from the cellar wall and flip it upside down until it was inverted beneath him.

Ghost glanced at the old man, begging for an explanation. But Mr. Crowley responded with a mere smile, his hands gesturing wildly as he prayed.

Ghost sensed the invisible strings holding him beginning to snap.

"Go into eternity, chosen one," Mr. Crowley commanded, ordering Ghost's body to float down toward the dagger-sharp tip of the cane. "Let this boy be the offering for thee."

It was then that Ghost realized the awful truth. He wasn't an acolyte of Mr. Crowley's ritual; he was a sacrifice. He struggled, wiggling like a speared fish as Mr. Crowley commanded his body toward the tip of the cane—about to impale him—when the doorbell rang.

Mr. Crowley's eyes snapped to the cellar door; his trance

completely severed. His eyes returned to Ghost as he dangled there helplessly in mid-air—his chore far from complete.

With a flick of his wrist, Mr. Crowley sent the cane back to the corner from whence it came. He held his hands over both of Ghost's ankles. With a mere touch, the deed was done. Ghost cried out in agony as his ankles snapped backward as if they were sticks of kindling. Mr. Crowley commanded his body to return to the ground where he set it down with all the tenderness of a parent.

Ghost quivered as he glanced down at his ankles, bones as white as moonlight jutting out from beneath the skin, dappled with flecks of red like rose petals. He would never be able to walk again. That much was certain. It was evident in the way the bones had broken, completely torn from their sockets and pulled out from beneath the skin by the old man.

Mr. Crowley swaddled Ghost in what felt like invisible twine—dressing him from head to toe until he was completely bound and could not move.

Although Ghost resisted as best he could, it was like struggling against piano wire—every move he made issued tiny cuts into his skin until his whole body was pocked with lines of blood.

Ghost flinched as Mr. Crowley regarded him with a promise—a promise that when he returned, he would bring more pain, more suffering if Ghost did not keep quiet. What else could he do but obey?

There was nothing Ghost could do but wait for Mr. Crowley to return, his body claimed by suffering and lost in a tide of pain that seemed hellbent to pull him further and further into a starless dark where all worshipped a God of agony.

CHAPTER TWENTY-NINE

Mr. Crowley appeared at the top of the cellar steps. Only this time, he wasn't alone. He was carrying the body of a man—the poor thing's face slashed and beaten in, his hair knotted with blood.

"What have you done to him?" Ghost cried out, a surge of anguish rocking him as he was reminded of his broken ankles. "You monster."

"We've been sent a gift, dear boy," Mr. Crowley explained, spreading the young man's body out against the floor. "Another offering for the ritual."

Ghost resisted, struggling against the invisible razor wire that Mr. Crowley had used to bind him.

"This was never about sending that—thing—back to wherever it came from," Ghost said, his voice trembling.

"You'll see, dear boy," the old man promised. "When I'm the great commander of the cosmos—when I'm the Creator of every living thing—you'll come to understand how a God should serve humanity."

Ghost glanced at the shape burned into the cellar wall, its smoldering edges beginning to fume with smoke and shimmer as if scabbed with starlight.

He watched as Mr. Crowley disrobed once more and hovered over both him and the body of the young man he had brought into the cellar. The old man began to recite another prayer in Latin.

Ghost's body shuddered as the floor began to shake. The nearby rows of worshippers seemed immune to the blast, their heads continually lowered and their lips moving with muted prayers.

He watched in silence as a blinding white light blared from the outline seared against the wall, spilling into the cellar and flooding the floor with mist. The ceiling cracked apart, debris scattering the floor as Mr. Crowley recited his prayer.

"Enter me, almighty force," Mr. Crowley commanded, closing his eyes. "Make me your vessel, eternal one, and make me invincible."

Mr. Crowley produced a knife and held it high above Ghost. The blade glistened in the deafening light, threatening to swallow him whole. Preparing for everything to go black, Ghost closed his eyes and waited for a moment. But nothing came. He was still alive. All sound around him had dimmed to silence.

He opened his eyes slowly and was greeted with the knife's blade pressing against his sternum. But holding the dagger back was something he hadn't anticipated seeing, something he hadn't ever expected to help him, something he could scarcely believe—the little spirit. The tiny creature was hovering above his chest, desperately clinging to Mr. Crowley's hand and peeling his fingers one by one away from the knife's handle until the creature sent it sailing from his grasp and clattering to the floor.

"What the fuck is this?" the old man asked.

Ghost swallowed. "You can see it?"

Although Mr. Crowley strained against the little spirit's pressure, it was no use. He watched helplessly as the tiny creature scampered up his arm and neared his face. Whether the old man opened his mouth to speak or to scream, Ghost was uncertain.

Regardless, it didn't matter.

The spirit took Mr. Crowley's face in both hands and began to inhale him—breathing in the black tar of his spirit until the old man began to shrink like a deflating balloon. Ghost watched in astonishment as the spirit gulped Mr. Crowley's entirety—the old man's skin pruning, his bones shortening, his eyes blackening and exploding like marshmallows held over a flame.

When all of his spirit had been drained by the ravenous little creature, Mr. Crowley had shrunken to the size of a dressmaker's thimble—his remaining essence now as tiny and as black as a worm thrown into a fire. Ghost watched as the creature that was once Mr. Crowley slithered away from the little spirit. He observed as the tiny slug made its way toward the shape burning in the cellar wall, as if it were still pursuing its now impossible quest—as if still determined to become God and taste the endlessness, the divinity of the cosmos.

Ghost reached out, swiping the creature from the wall where it tried to hide and held it in his hands. The slug cowered, its tail curling at the sight of Ghost and writhing back and forth in the center of Ghost's open palm. For a moment, Ghost pitied him. The poor thing—scared, defenseless, a tiny monster.

After all, that's what Ghost had been.

No. Perhaps he was capable of more than that. Perhaps he was endowed with gifts—special things—that made him more than a mere monster. The little spirit had proven that to him. It wasn't a parasite—it was his protector.

He thought of such things as he closed his palm tightly and squished the life out of the tiny black slug until it was smeared along the palm of his hand like toothpaste.

He wiped his hand against the ground and turned to the body of the young man Mr. Crowley had brought to the cellar. He was still breathing. Barely.

Something pulled his peripheral vision away from the poor man—a white light calling to him, a voice telling him not to be afraid.

When Ghost looked up, he found the ceiling of the cellar had been ripped apart—constellations swirling in the space between and white light pooling there.

A giant glowing orb hung where the ceiling had been blown away, the outline of the body seared into the wall was now washed in light and dripping specks of ash that circled Ghost and began to blanket him like a snow squall.

Ghost opened his mouth to speak, but only light seemed to dribble from between his lips. There was a faint hum rumbling in the pit of his gut—confessions aching to be admitted, secrets longing to be told. But he had no voice to release them. It was as if the light emanating from inside him had paralyzed his vocal cords to keep him from speaking.

It was then he realized he didn't require a voice to speak to the glowing white orb as it swayed there. They could speak to one another through telepathy.

Ghost sensed his insides warming as the light thanked him. Then, it asked him what he wanted most in return for his sacrifice.

Ghost's mind slowed for a moment. Of course, he thought of his beloved Hailey—the light of his life, the light of all lights. But he was instantly reminded of more pressing matters as the body of the young man—"Malik. His name's Malik," the light had told to him—lying beside him on the floor and leaking blood everywhere.

Ghost swallowed hard. He knew in his heart what he had to choose.

He asked God to spare Malik—to stop his bleeding and reach inside his mind to confiscate every horrible memory of his suffering.

The white light vibrated, seeming to ask if Ghost was sure of his decision.

Ghost didn't even hesitate.

"Yes," he silently told the light.

Malik's limp body was lifted from the ground and held in the air for a moment—dangling there and floating as if held by a pair of invisible hands. Ghost watched, mouth open in disbelief, as Malik rotated there on an unseen coil—ash-like embers swirling around him in a flurry. He watched as Malik's blood dried and the holes in his abdomen closed until it was as if they had never been there.

He watched as a pool of light entered Malik's head and drained him of his thoughts until his face softened with contentment. His whole body shuddered, as if mourning the loss of his suffering—bereaving the demise of his agony.

In the way that all dreamers can travel far distances and look into distant homes, private lives—God transported Ghost to Malik's home. Malik had been delivered to the couch—his clothes cleaned, his hair combed, and a smile etched into his face in the way that the lobotomized are supposedly calmed. There, sitting beside him, was his husband Brett. Neither one appeared troubled, as if they were effigies of their former selves. They were content, forever smiling, their minds emptied of such indescribable pain and suffering—a young couple eternally in love.

Brett grabbed Malik's arm, gasping for air as if finally surfacing from being held underwater for too long.

"I was so scared," Brett told his husband, coughing as he spoke.

"Of what?" Malik asked.

Tears lifted from Brett's cheeks like beads of morning dew, spiraling into the air until they floated away. "I—don't remember."

"Me neither."

Malik seemed to soften—as if glad he couldn't remember, as if delighted that whatever had been taken from him was now permanently gone.

He didn't need it anymore.

Ghost watched them both for a moment, admiring their affection for one another and wishing he could have the same. When he was content with what he had done, he was returned to the cellar of Mr. Crowley's house and the basement was as it was before the ritual. The ceiling had been repaired, the blood on the floor had been dried—it was as if none of the disasters had ever occurred.

Ghost observed without comment as the worshippers rose from their kneeling positions, heads swiveling all around, desperate to understand where they were and what had happened to them.

He saw Gemma rise from her place.

They immediately locked eyes and he was pleased to see her memory of him had not yet faded.

She hastened to his side and begged him for an explanation. But Ghost found himself struggling to speak—as if his throat was closing, as if something had willed him to be silent. She pushed herself into the corner of his armpit and closed her eyes, thanking her protector. He accepted her kindness without comment, stroking her hair and pulling her a little closer.

Ghost knew in his heart that there were no words to summarize the horrible misfortunes they had endured. Still, as the others began to carry him up the stairs and out of the dark cellar, he hoped that Gemma might one day listen to him and all the words he might try to invent to describe the horror they had lived through—the evil they had forever undone.

A FINAL HYMN THAT ONLY GHOSTS CAN HEAR

Late in the month of December, Ghost called for a taxi and ordered the driver to take him to a house on Elizabeth Street—the place where Malik and Brett lived. He wasn't sure why he so desperately needed to visit them—he wasn't even sure what he would do if he found out they were home. After all, how could Malik possibly remember him? God had made it so that all of his former agony had been wiped from him. All Ghost knew was that he wanted to see them again, wanted to see the life he had returned to them and the happiness with which he had blessed them.

As the cab slowed and pulled onto the shoulder of the road in front of the small house, Ghost watched as a moving van idled in the driveway—a group of men bundled in coats ferrying large boxes from the house and loading them into the rear of the vehicle. It was then he noticed Malik and Brett standing on the front porch holding one another closely, as they silently observed the movers empty their home.

Ghost thought of climbing out of the car—wheeling himself up the front pathway and introducing himself to them, telling them what he had done and how he had saved them both. But he reasoned they didn't need to know. They didn't need to be reminded of the horrors they had once endured—horrors that had threatened to destroy them. Ghost found himself content with simply watching them—seeing the hope glimmer in their eyes as they seemed to look ahead towards their future with open arms.

Ordering the driver to drive on, the cab pulled away from the curb and sped down the lane. Perhaps once upon a time, Ghost might have sought the comfort—the validation—from them. But it no longer mattered to him. All that mattered now was that they had been saved, any unpleasantness erased from their memory. They were free to start over. That was all Ghost had wanted for them.

On Christmas morning, Ghost spent the day with Gemma and her daughter, Piper. They sang carols, drank hot chocolate, and watched cartoons before finally opening presents.

For once, Ghost felt less alone. He felt like less of a monster.

Of course, there were moments when the thoughts would creep up on him and remind him of all he had lost—when the little spirit around his neck would make its presence known to him—but those moments seemed to become fewer and further between whenever he spent time with Gemma's daughter. In his quietest moments of despair, he was reminded of the affection Piper held for him whenever she was near—the love that she returned to him in spades, for the father she'd never had.

He watched as she played with her gifts, reveling in the moment he had longed for—a family.

His enjoyment was short-lived, as he suddenly noticed a tiny hand—as delicate and as finely woven as lace—curl itself around the little girl's throat. There, perched on her shoulder, was a little spirit much like the one that had claimed him long ago.

Ghost wondered how this could have happened. Had he somehow poisoned her? Had he infected her with the same wraith of guilt that possessed him so many years ago? He couldn't be certain.

Piper seemed unbothered by the tiny wraith as it desperately clung to her, occasionally feeding from her. Whether she knew it was there and just wasn't concerned, Ghost couldn't be sure. Whether it was something only Ghost could see, he wasn't certain. He merely watched in silence as the spirit floated around the little girl's head, its tail of smoke coiled around her neck, delicately woven into her skin.

In the past he might have whitened at the sight, might have warned her mother or done something unreasonable to try and save her from the little creature. But he was glad to see it—glad to know she was protected and would be safe from all harm that might come her way. Of course, in turn, she would have to give little parts of herself to the spirit—she'd have to make small offerings of herself, things she might never want to share. Ghost knew that when the time came— when she was older and prepared to accept the responsibility—he would share with her everything he knew. Every trick he had learned, every means he had used to cope—all of it would be hers.

He knew that in time she would not be afraid and would come to understand how and why it was truly wondrous.

THE END

ACKNOWLEDGMENTS

I began writing the first draft of what would become *Everything the Darkness Eats* in January of 2021. There are many kind souls to whom I'm indebted. Without their support, this novel surely would not exist.

First, my heartfelt gratitude belongs to my mother. I delivered her a freshly completed chapter almost every night for an entire month and she never wavered in her support or interest. Her dedication truly motivated me to finish this book despite the incessant chattering of self-doubt inside my mind.

Next, of course, my beloved partner, Ali. He remains my greatest advocate and always encourages me to be fearless when I write.

I owe so much gratitude to my editors, Christoph Paul and Leza Cantoral, for their unwavering love and devotion throughout the grueling process of publishing a novel—especially a *debut* novel. I'll never forget Christoph's excitement after he read one of the many drafts of this book and told me how much it reminded him of when he first discovered Clive Barker's *The Damnation Game*. I cherish that wonderful memory to this day.

I extend all my love and thankfulness to my literary agent, Priya Doraswamy, and my Film/TV manager, Ryan Lewis.

Finally, I sincerely thank you, dear reader, for meeting me in the darkness. I've guided you far enough. It's your turn to find your own way...

Eric LaRocca (*he/they*) is the Bram Stoker Award®-nominated author of several works of horror and dark fiction, including the viral sensation, *Things Have Gotten Worse Since We Last Spoke*. A lover of luxury fashion and an admirer of European musical theatre, Eric can often be found roaming the streets of his home city, Boston, MA, for inspiration. For more information, please follow @hystericteeth on Twitter/Instagram or visit ericlarocca.com.

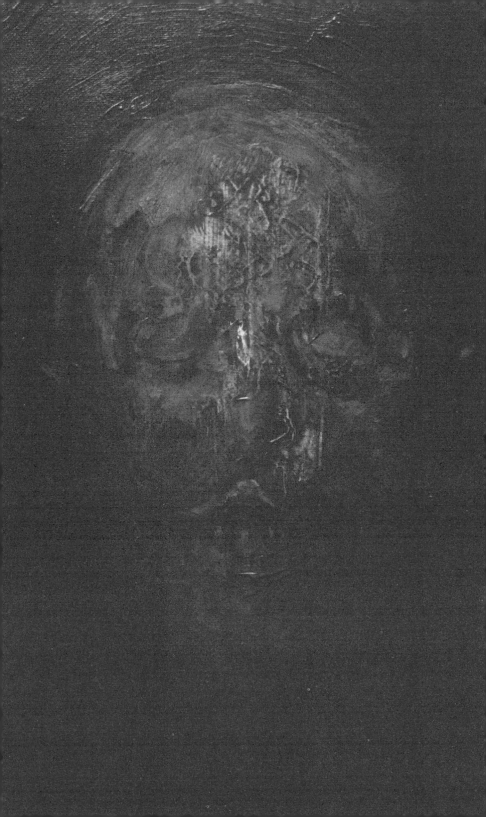